Cloaked in Red

YA
VANDE
VALDE,
VIVIAN
C.2

Text copyright © 2010 by Vande Velde, Vivian
Photographs by Shutterstock

Website: www.marshallcavendish.us/kids

This book is a work of fiction. Names, characters, places, and incidents are products of the author's imagination and are used fictitiously. Any resemblance to actual events or locales or persons, living or dead, is entirely coincidental.

Other Marshall Cavendish Offices:
Marshall Cavendish International (Asia) Private Limited, 1 New Industrial Road, Singapore 536196 • Marshall Cavendish International (Thailand) Co Ltd. 253 Asoke, 12th Flr, Sukhumvit 21 Road, Klongtoey Nua, Wattana, Bangkok 10110, Thailand • Marshall Cavendish (Malaysia) Sdn Bhd, Times Subang, Lot 46, Subang Hi-Tech Industrial Park, Batu Tiga, 40000 Shah Alam, Selangor Darul Ehsan, Malaysia

Marshall Cavendish is a trademark of Times Publishing Limited

Library of Congress Cataloging-in-Publication Data

Vande Velde, Vivian.
Cloaked in red / by Vivian Vande Velde. — 1st ed.
v. cm.
Summary: Presents eight twists on the traditional tale of Little Red Riding Hood, exploring such issues as why most characters seem dim-witted and what, exactly, is the theme.
Contents: The red cloak — The red riding hood doll — Little Red Riding Hood's family — Granny and the wolf — Deems the wood gatherer — Why Willy and his brother will never amount to anything — The little red headache — Little Red Riding Hood's little red riding hood.
ISBN 978-0-7614-5793-0
1. Fairy tales—United States. 2. Children's stories, American. [1. Fairy tales. 2. Humorous stories. 3. Short stories.] I. Little Red Riding Hood. English. II. Title.
PZ8.V2374Clo 2010
[Fic]—dc22
2009051753

Book design by Becky Terhune
Editor: Margery Cuyler

Printed in China (E)
First edition
10 9 8 7 6 5 4 3
mc Marshall Cavendish

To Beth and Josh—
wishing you happy ever after

Cloaked in Red

VIVIAN VANDE VELDE

Marshall Cavendish

Table of Contents

Author's Note

8

The Red Cloak

16

The Red Riding Hood Doll

32

Little Red Riding Hood's Family

48

Granny and the Wolf

58

Deems the Wood Gatherer

81

Why Willy and His Brother Won't Ever Amount to Anything

92

The Little Red Headache

100

Little Red Riding Hood's Little Red Riding Hood

109

AUTHOR'S NOTE

Everyone knows the story of Little Red Riding Hood, the girl with the unfortunate name and the inability to tell the difference between her grandmother and a member of a different species.

The question is: *Why* do we all know it?

If you look at "Little Red Riding Hood," it's a perfect example of the exact opposite of a good story.

There are different versions, but they all start with a mother who sends her daughter into the woods, where there is not only a wolf, but a talking, cross-dressing wolf. We are never told Little Red Riding Hood's age, but her actions clearly show that she is much too young, or too dimwitted, to be allowed out of the house alone.

But apparently Little Red's mom hasn't noticed this.

When I was a little girl, my mother was nervous about my crossing the street without adult supervision. But fairy-tale characters do not make good role models. Goldilocks' parents not only let her play in the bear-infested woods, they neglect to give her that most basic advice: "Don't break into strangers' homes."

There are other examples of irresponsible adults in fairy tales. The miller in "Rumpelstiltskin" hands his daughter over to a king whose royal motto is "Spin straw into gold or die." And Rapunzel's mom and dad trade her to a witch for a garden salad.

We won't even get into the issue of stepmothers.

So, Mother tells Little Red not to tarry or to talk to strangers. (Not talking: That'll be a big help against wolves.) Why can't Mother deliver the basket of food to Granny herself rather than send a child through dangerous woods into a house with a possibly contagious disease? Maybe Mother is *trying* to get rid of her daughter. Maybe this is the same mother who tried to lose Hansel and Gretel in the woods. Little Red Riding Hood's peculiar name might make more sense in this light. I can just picture the father—not that he ever makes an appearance in this story—putting his foot down, saying, "Geez Louise! You name our first kid Hansel. You name our second kid Gretel. I'm not letting you name any more kids. We'll just call our youngest daughter after an article of clothing."

How would you feel if your parents called you "Little Blue-Plaid Catholic School Uniform" or "Little Green Sweatshirt with the Hole at the Elbow"?

And what happened later in life, when Little Red Riding Hood was no longer little? Did she shift to "Medium-Sized Blue-Beaded Sweater"? Did she eventually become "Size-Large and Yes-That-DOES-Make-Your-Butt-Look-Enormous Jeans"?

Does Little Red resent her name? We don't know enough about her to say.

We don't know enough about the wolf, once he comes along, to know why he acts the way he acts. If the wolf were hungry, you'd expect him to just go ahead and eat the girl. But maybe he figures it's rude to eat someone to whom he hasn't been introduced, so when he sees Little Red Riding Hood in the woods picking flowers, he starts asking her questions.

Apparently Little Red is quite a conversationalist, because the next thing you know, the wolf has learned everything there is to know about the child, including directions to her granny's house. Still, Little Red is not suspicious when the wolf tells her, "You go this way, and I'll go that, and we'll see who gets there first."

See what I mean about young or dimwitted?

So Little Red takes the long way, and the wolf takes the shortcut, running ahead to Granny's.

Here's where the different versions come in.

In some tellings, the wolf locks Granny in the closet—not behavior you're ever likely to see on a *National Geographic* special.

In other accounts, the wolf eats the grandmother, in which case you'd expect Little Red, on her arrival, to notice subtle clues—maybe bits of shredded clothing or gnawed-on bones or blood splatters. But maybe Granny is not a careful housekeeper, and a certain amount of mess is normal for her house.

And sometimes the wolf swallows Granny whole, in which case the wolf must be about as big as a whale, leaving us to wonder why Little Red, who seems prone to making personal remarks, doesn't mention this.

In any case, then the wolf gets into Granny's bed—which sounds kinky to me regardless of *what* he's done with her previously.

Along comes Little Red.

I don't like to criticize anyone's family, but I'm guessing these people are not what you'd call close. Little Red doesn't realize a wolf has substituted himself for her grandmother. I only met my grandmother three times in my entire life, but I like to think I would have noticed if someone claiming to be my grandmother had fur, fangs, and a tail.

But Little Red, instead of becoming suspicious, becomes rude.

"My," she says—as far as she knows—to her grandmother, "what big arms you have."

Big she notices. Apparently *hairy* and *clawed* escape her.

The wolf answers, "The better to hug you with, my dear."

Aw, how sweet. You'd think that would warm Little Red's heart. But no.

"My," she goes on, "what big eyes you have."

"The better to see you with, my dear," the wolf answers.

(Are you wondering what he's waiting for? *I'm* wondering what he's waiting for.)

"My," Little Red Riding Hood says, "what great big teeth you have."

What would the wolf have done if Little Red Riding Hood had commented on his whiskers or his snout, or if she had simply handed over the basket of goodies? Just how long would he have kept up the impersonation?

But either the wolf's just a big joker who has been patiently waiting for the perfect cue to what he knows is a killer punch line, or he's sensitive about his dental appearance. At this point he answers, "The better to eat you with," then leaps out of bed and lunges at Little Red Riding Hood.

The story doesn't specify whether the child catches on that she has been chatting all this while with a wolf, or if she simply thinks her grandmother is extremely cranky. But at least Little Red finally realizes that something is wrong—and for that we can only be grateful.

What happens next depends once again on which version you're reading.

Shortest: The wolf eats Little Red. The end.

More often, Little Red screams and a friendly woodcutter happens by. Well, friendly to Little Red, not to the wolf.

The woodcutter either scares the wolf off or escalates from *wood*cutter into *wolf*cutter: He cuts the wolf open and out pops Granny. (Presumably she's all slimy with wolf's blood and digestive juices, which you'd think would emotionally traumatize any normal little girl. Then again, there's never any strong evidence Little Red is normal. On the other hand, maybe the reason there's never any mention of Little Red in therapy is because there aren't very many support groups for those who have witnessed family members rescued from the inside of carnivores.)

In the less messy versions, the woodcutter kills the wolf, and afterwards he lets Granny out of the closet. Of course, this leaves us with the question: If Granny were alive and well in the closet, why didn't she say anything when her granddaughter was struggling with the difference between a beast of the forest and a family member? You know, something to end Little Red's confusion. Perhaps something like: "RUN, YOU LITTLE DIPSTICK, BEFORE HE EATS YOU!"

In the oldest written telling of the story, not to mention the most bizarre, the wolf swallows both Granny and Little Red whole, then decides to take an after-dinner nap. The woodcutter comes into Granny's cottage (we can only guess at the relationship that makes him feel at home doing this), and he sees the wolf's bulging stomach (earning him the "Most Observant Character in This Story" Award). He slices open the wolf, releasing the grateful, if icky, girl and grandmother. Apparently, the woodcutter is a skilled surgeon, because this procedure not only doesn't kill the wolf; it also doesn't wake

..... up. Then, in a scene that sounds right out of one of those sadistic slasher movies, the woodcutter, Granny, and Little Red fill the wolf's stomach with stones, and then they sew him up. Apparently these three are too kindhearted to kill the wolf in his sleep. This way, once he wakes up and tries to jump out of bed, the weight of the stones in his tummy rips him apart. *Eeeewww!*

Okay, think about all this. What makes a good story?

1. Memorable characters

We've got a mother, Little Red Riding Hood, a wolf, a grandmother, and a woodcutter. It's hard to call characters memorable when the only one who has a name is, in fact, named after apparel that nobody wears anymore.

2. Vivid setting

The woods. Okay, are we talking Amazon rain forest here or a couple of trees in someone's backyard? It's sloppy storytelling if we aren't given enough information to picture *where* our memorable characters are.

3. Exciting plot

Try submitting a story to your creative writing teacher in which the main character bumbles cluelessly throughout the story, then gets rescued by another character who was never even mentioned before. Go ahead and keep your fingers crossed for a passing grade.

4. Important themes—something about the subject to

captivate our imaginations and connect with those who read the story.

It's hard to determine the theme of "Little Red Riding Hood." Don't go into the woods? Don't talk to animals who are capable of talking back? If you're going to make fun of your grandmother's appearance, make sure it truly *is* your grandmother and not a wolf who likes to dress in old-ladies' clothes?

However you look at it, "Little Red Riding Hood" is a strange and disturbing story that should probably *not* be shared with children.

That is why I've gone ahead and written eight new versions of it.

The Red Cloak

Once upon a time, after fashion was discovered but before people had makeovers on TV, there was a young girl named Meg.

Meg was a mousy girl with hair that was somewhere between too short and too long, somewhere between straight and limp, somewhere between without shine and downright drab. Her eyes were a color that was not quite brown or tan, something like earth that is too dry. The only thing that could be said about her eyes was that she didn't need glasses—which was fortunate since this was before glasses had been invented.

So poor eyesight wasn't the reason Meg's clothes were dull and plain. Truth be told, Meg didn't care about such things as being stylish because she believed that most people didn't even notice her.

She was right.

Meg was a shy, quiet girl who liked to daydream about being somewhere else, or sometimes, when her dreams were big, someone else. Her daydreams easily distracted her from the chores her mother asked her to do—such as weeding the garden—and instead she would spend the day watching parent robins gather twigs to build their nests, or she would wonder how flower nectar tasted to butterflies, or she would get caught up in listening to the song of the crickets.

One spring day, Meg came home after a morning of not-quite-gardening, and she discovered that her mother had taken her favorite cloak, which was the dusty color of moths' wings, and dyed it bright red.

"Oh," Meg said, "that's . . ." She tried to think of another word for horrible, besides ghastly. "That's . . . quite a change." She thought the color screamed LOOK AT ME, and Meg was not a look-at-me kind of girl.

"Yes, it is nice, isn't it?" Meg's mother said as she swung the cloak around Meg's shoulders and tied it at her throat. "Red is my favorite color."

Meg was too polite to make choking noises or to say more than, "I know it is."

Meg's mother said, "It was when I was wearing my own beautiful red dress that I'd woven and sewn for the harvest festival that your father first noticed me. He came right up and asked me to dance. We danced and danced. Such a handsome young man he was. Before the night was over, I realized he was my one true love." This was Meg's mother's favorite story. Depending on how much time there was for other details, the story always ended, "And we lived happily ever after."

Surely, Meg had thought from a very young age, *there's more to falling in love and living happily ever after than a pretty red dress.*

But once, when Meg had pointed that out to her mother, her mother had said, "Nobody likes an argumentative child, dear." And when she'd asked her father, he'd mumbled and grumbled into the bowl of porridge he'd been eating and said, "Men don't know about that sort of thing. Ask your mother."

So now here was Meg, with her nice, safe, gray cloak dyed look-at-me red, and all Meg could think was that she was glad this was spring, not fall. At least there were five months to go before the next harvest dance, for although Meg liked the idea of finding her one true love and marrying him and living happily ever after, the idea of *boys* was kind of scary.

"Well," said Meg to her mother, so flustered she couldn't remember if she'd said it already, "thank you very much."

Meanwhile, she was thinking, *It's May. The nights don't get THAT cold anymore. I probably won't need—not absolutely NEED—a cloak till September or October.*

But some people only hear what they want to hear. Her

mother said, "I'm so glad you like my little surprise."

"Surprise," Meg repeated. "Yes, this is . . . definitely . . . a surprise."

"Good," Meg's mother said. "And your grandmother will love to see it."

Meg nodded. She knew her grandmother loved her, and would continue to love her no matter what Meg was wearing. Her grandmother had seen her in *diapers*. Her grandmother had seen her without diapers, for goodness' sakes. Meg could stand to look foolish in front of her grandmother.

"Is Grandmother coming here tonight?" Meg asked. She could put the cloak away with the winter clothes tomorrow.

"No," Meg's mother said. "You go and visit her now. I'm so excited, I can't wait for her to see you." And, sure enough, her voice was getting high and squeaky with anticipation.

Meg and her parents lived on the outskirts of the village of Aberwold, and so did Grandmother. Unfortunately, Grandmother didn't live on the same outskirts—she lived way over on the far side of the village. Meg thought of having to walk through the streets of Aberwold, with everyone laughing at her in her outrageous red cloak.

"Oh," Meg said, "surely it would be rude to just drop in on Grandmother."

"Nonsense," her mother answered. "Grandmothers love to

see their granddaughters. Besides. . . ." Meg's mother glanced around the room. "Besides . . . I need you to take her . . . something."

"What?" Meg demanded, suspicious that her mother was making this up as she went along.

Meg's mother snatched up a wooden bowl. "This. I need you to take her this."

Meg said, "She loaned you that at Christmastime, when she gave us that chicken stew."

"Yes," said Meg's mother, "and it's high time we returned it."

"But . . ." Meg said as her mother put the bowl into her hands. "But . . ."

Her mother gently but firmly pushed Meg backwards, backwards, until she forced Meg out the door.

"But . . ."

Her mother closed the door in her face.

Meg considered going out to the garden. Nobody would see her there. Animals don't worry about fashion—unless it's fur.

But her mother was so pleased with herself because of that silly red monstrosity.

The cloak felt hotter than it had when it had been gray. And itchier.

There's no way, Meg thought, *I'm walking through the center of the village looking like a gigantic strolling strawberry.*

All right, that was one decision made. Now, Meg had two choices:

1. She could take the cloak off and carry it while she walked to her grandmother's house.

2. She could go a different route that didn't cut directly through Aberwold but went along the outside edges.

Although Meg liked the idea of taking the cloak off, she didn't like the idea of carrying it. She was already toting that silly bowl. Besides, beneath the cloak she was wearing her gardening clothes. They were the exact opposite of the show-offy cloak, but not in a good way. They were so shabby and tattered and stained that, in the end, they too called attention to themselves.

Choice number two was better because, though it would take longer to walk around the outside of the village, there would be fewer people for Meg to run into. Half of Aberwold's population gathered daily in the village square to do their buying and selling and gossiping, which was precisely why Meg didn't want to go there. The closer she kept to the outskirts of Aberwold, the fewer people she would see—or would see her.

So that was the choice Meg favored, until she came up with an even better choice, a variation on choice number two:

2 (modified). She could avoid even more people by walking—not on the outskirts of the village—but outside the village entirely: in the encircling woods.

Of course, her parents claimed the woods were dangerous and said she should not venture there unless one of them was with her. But Meg thought that was just because of the infuriating way adults had of making a big deal out of everything. Adults liked to say "Act grown up" and then turn around and say, "You're just a child."

Meg started down the path that led into the heart of the village, aware that her mother was at the window, watching and waving.

The path turned left, and Meg turned left. But she only took a dozen steps before she veered off the path and went toward the right, where the trees grew thickly.

I will only walk a little bit into the woods, Meg told herself. *Just deep enough for no one to be able to see me.*

But through the trees she glimpsed their nosey neighbor, Goody Dorcas, hanging some clothes out on the line to dry. Meg went farther into the woods, because if Goody Dorcas were to glimpse *her*, Meg's mother would hear of it before the afternoon was over.

And then Meg went farther still into the woods after she heard some children, probably little Elinor and Kate, playing and squealing with laughter in their yard.

And farther again where she heard a dog barking, because she grew afraid someone would come out to investigate what the dog was barking at.

The woods were not silent. Meg could hear birds. She could hear rustlings of what she sincerely hoped were *little* creatures in the underbrush. She could hear the buzz of insects.

There was no real path, only trees that were very close together, or far enough apart for her to squeeze through. Branches caught her red cloak, her hair, her arms.

When Meg felt she had gone far enough, she cut back toward the village and found she had not walked nearly the distance she had thought. She heard the metallic clang from the workshop of Almost-Toothless Tom, the blacksmith. She wasn't even halfway to her grandmother's. She ducked back into the woods before anyone could see her.

She walked and walked and walked. Some persistent insect wanted to burrow into her hair. The cloak was hot, the bowl was heavy. Already unhappy, she became aware that the bowl still smelled, very faintly, of the stew it had been used for— which reminded Meg that she had gone into her house for lunch, but left without eating. She was sure that these were the reasons time and distance seemed to be moving so slowly, so she kept on walking and let her thoughts drift, like motes in a sunbeam.

Why hadn't she had the courage to speak out? Yes, her mother would have been disappointed if Meg had said that she hated the red color and that she wouldn't wear the cloak again until Mother dyed it back to its own soggy oatmeal color. But Mother would not have died of a broken heart over it.

When Meg finally turned once more toward Aberwold, Aberwold wasn't there.

In her worry about being seen from people's back yards, Meg thought at first that she must have angled farther away than she had meant to.

But then she thought she must have overshot the village entirely.

And then, finally, she thought: *I'm lost.*

Surely Aberwold was back here somewhere, either to the right or to the left. But the farther Meg walked, the closer together the trees seemed to grow, and that compelled her to go in the one direction she was fairly certain she did not want to go.

Those underbrush rattlings she'd been hearing seemed to get noisier. *Just your imagination,* Meg assured herself, and she forced her mind *not* to wander. Until she stepped between two trees and found herself facing a wolf.

Mostly, she tried to tell herself, *wolves don't attack people.* Mostly.

The wolf stared at her with its golden-yellow eyes, lowered its ears, and pulled its lips into a snarl, showing its many sharp teeth.

Meg took a step back.

Wolves generally travel in packs. Did that mean there were more nearby? More wolves, who would feel this section of the woods was their territory, and that they must defend their territory from her?

Meg took another step back. She could no longer see the wolf, though she realized the wolf probably could still see her, since she was so much taller. No doubt it heard her, too. She must try to breathe more quietly, though with its keen nose, it would be able to smell her. The wolf could easily track her, if that's what it wanted to do.

Meg stumbled on a tree root and nearly fell. Walking backwards in the woods was surely almost as dangerous as turning one's back on a wolf.

Still . . . *Don't run,* Meg told herself. *Don't let it know you're afraid,* although it could probably smell her fear, too.

Meg moved as briskly as she could through the trees that offered the least resistance. In her imagination, the wolf was right behind her, about to leap onto her back with claws and fangs. Meg kept whipping around—not that facing a wolf would offer much protection. What could she do? Throw her grandmother's bowl at its head? So far there was no sign that the wolf was following her.

Which didn't, of course, mean it wasn't.

From up ahead she heard a noise.

More wolves?

No, she realized, it wasn't an animal noise; it was a people noise. It was the sound of someone chopping wood.

Meg rushed forward, convinced that the wolf was going to attack now, when help seemed just footsteps away. She could only hope that whoever it was would come to her aid when she started screaming. On the other hand, there was an equal chance, she guessed, that she might scare a would-be rescuer away.

Meg burst into a little clearing that she had not passed through before. A man with an ax was chopping away at the trunk of a tree.

"Help!" she called.

Startled, the woodcutter looked up. "The tree was struck by lightning," he said. "It was already half fallen over. I'm just taking the broken bits off. All through!" He tossed his ax into a small cart that would help him transport the wood back to the village, as if she wouldn't notice how much wood he already had, or the ax marks in the trunk of the tree that was still standing, though tilting.

Meg knew that woodcutters weren't actually supposed to take down trees. Forests belonged to the king, and people were only allowed to take what had been knocked off by nature.

Not that Meg was going to be a stickler for rules in a situation like this.

"That's all right," Meg said. "I don't care. I'm lost, and there's a wolf nearby. Please help me get home."

The woodcutter stepped beyond her in the direction from which she had come. He sniffed, as though he could smell wolves as easily as wolves could smell people. He shook his head. "If there was a wolf, it's gone now. More likely, it was a dog that frightened you. We're close to the north end of Aberwold."

Meg didn't argue that she knew the difference between a wolf and a dog. North Aberwold was good. North Aberwold was where her grandmother lived. Though, at this point, *any* Aberwold was good. "Still," Meg said, "I've lost my way. May I follow you back?"

The man nodded, but he looked as if he were thinking, rather than answering her. "My," he said, "what a fine red cloak you have."

Meg didn't know how to answer that.

"Looks real rich."

Meg didn't know how to answer that, either.

"Your parents rich, girl?"

"No," Meg said.

"Rich enough to afford to give me a reward for finding you and rescuing you?"

Meg thought of offering him the cloak, since he seemed so taken with it. But she suspected he was more interested in hard cash. She said, "My parents don't have much money. This is an old cloak, just newly dyed." She held up the edge, which was more frayed than ever since her journey through the woods.

"I'm sure they'll be able to come up with something," he said, "after you've been gone a day or two."

"But I've been gone only since noon," she pointed out.

The woodcutter grinned at her. "That can change."

Meg saw all sorts of problems with the man's plan. Even if her parents *were* rich, they would not reward him after she told them he had intentionally kept her away from them in order to collect a reward. How did he intend to keep her from telling them that? How did he intend to keep her from telling everyone that he'd been illegally chopping down trees? Meg worried that it wasn't that he had not thought of these problems. Rather, she suspected, he intended to overcome the shortcomings of his plan by taking measures to ensure she wouldn't tell anyone anything.

Were they close enough to Aberwold that someone would hear her if she cried for help? Surely this woodcutter had walked far enough from the village that people couldn't hear him chopping away at the trees. Was a scream louder than a chop?

Meg decided to take her chances. "Here," she said, and tossed him her grandmother's bowl. Then, while he was busy looking at it, no doubt wondering *why* she had thrown it to him, she flung her head back and gave a long wolf howl.

"My," the woodcutter said, "what a loud voice you have. But no one can hear you."

Maybe no humans, but she hoped a territorial wolf would consider her howl a challenge, a wolf such as the one she'd met earlier, whose attention—she'd suddenly realized—had come from smelling Grandmother's stew in the pores of the wooden bowl she'd been carrying.

And in a moment a wolf—whether it was the same she had already seen or a different one—stepped into the little clearing.

"I think you'd better drop that bowl," Meg advised.

The woodcutter did. Then he said, "You're closer to the cart. Hand me the ax," since the wolf was standing between him and the cart, where he'd put his ax.

"No," Meg said. "I don't think so. My, what big teeth that wolf has. Maybe you'd better try to frighten it away."

"Shoo!" the woodcutter said, as if the wolf were a pesky barnyard chicken.

The wolf didn't look as if it enjoyed being shooed. It flattened its ears and stepped toward the woodcutter.

Since figuring things out didn't seem the man's greatest strength, Meg said, "I don't think you can scare it, and I don't think you can outrun it. Perhaps you'd better climb a tree."

Instead, the woodcutter stamped his foot, as if he were

about to lunge at the wolf, and he flapped his arms and half growled, half yelled, "Ya!"

Apparently the wolf was no more fond of that than it was of being treated like a chicken. It lunged—and it was not pretend lunging. The woodcutter ran for the nearest tree. By unhappy coincidence, that was the one he'd been chopping down. The gash he'd made with his ax offered a good foothold for climbing, but once the man had shimmied up the trunk, it began to sway.

Meg yelled up at him, "You probably should move as little as possible."

The wolf went over to the dropped bowl and ran its tongue around the inside surface. Then it crouched down at the base of the tree and looked up at the woodcutter.

"I'll get help," Meg volunteered. She resisted the impulse to suggest that she might be due a reward for rescuing him. Very slowly, she backed away from the wolf, but the creature seemed more interested in the woodcutter than in her. She felt guilty, because she knew the bowl had attracted the wolf's attention, but—all things considered—she did not feel guilty enough to regret what she'd done.

Meg followed the tracks the man and his cart had made coming into the woods, and in no time at all, she could hear the sounds of village life. She walked through the trees and found herself very close to her grandmother's house.

She thought: *I've stared down a wolf, and outsmarted a*

man who wanted to hold me for ransom, and found my way to grandmother's after being lost in the woods. Surely I can find the courage to tell my mother I don't want my cloak to be red. A group of village boys walked by her, and one of them, a fine-looking young man named Jack, turned back to smile at her.

On the other hand, Meg thought, standing just a little bit straighter and a little bit taller in her red cloak, *there's no reason to be hasty.*

The Red Riding Hood Doll

Once upon a time, before department stores and designer labels, there was a young seamstress named Georgette. Georgette lived and worked with her mother, both of them fashioning beautiful dresses for rich ladies who would wear those dresses to elegant parties that Georgette and her mother were never invited to.

Georgette told herself she didn't care about the parties; she was much too busy to attend in any case. There was always measuring and cutting and sewing and tatting lace and attaching beads, not to mention ripping out seams and starting all over again for a client who had eaten too much at the last party or two or three. Many was the time Georgette worked long into the night, since many of her customers ordered their dresses at the last minute after finding out what the most important ladies were going to be wearing.

So Georgette didn't feel bad about not going to the parties, which, in any case, her mother said were not for the likes of her. She didn't feel bad about not having a husband, since her mother had pointed out often enough that Georgette was too plain and set in her ways to attract a man. But Georgette missed a child to love, a child who would make *her* feel loved in return. Georgette was quietly sure she would be a better mother than her own mother had been.

Georgette's mother said, "I think you'd do better to get a cat instead a child. Cats are less trouble," which didn't do much to help Georgette in the feeling-loved department.

One day, Georgette stayed up for two nights working on a red satin cloak with an ermine fur-trimmed hood for a woman who was significantly bigger than she had insisted she was. There had been many last-moment alterations, and the client now refused to accept the cloak and pay for it.

"First of all," the lady said, "that cloak is much too large. I can see *that* without even trying it on. I asked you to make it a smidgen more generous, since you cut it too stingily last time, and you've gone and made it huge. The cloak was to be for *me*, not my horse. I don't know what you were thinking, because now there isn't time to alter it before Lord Randolph's riding party. And what have you gone and done to the color? That is much too vibrant a red, and it will make me look sallow. I don't think that's the fabric I selected at all. I think you've gone and substituted another measure of cloth for the one I chose—no doubt a cheaper material. You tradespeople always have your tricks to try to take advantage."

Georgette had worked on garments for this particular lady before, and she knew who was trying to take advantage of whom.

The lady sighed, many times, but she couldn't stop running her fingers over the material, that was so smooth and cool it felt like water, and over Georgette's stitches that were tiny and perfectly even.

Georgette wished her mother would say something in her defense. Something like: "It's not the cloak that's too large; it's your big, ugly behind that's too large." Or: "Of course that's the fabric you selected. We were just too polite to tell you that you're too old to wear such a bright shade of red, but we *did* try to talk you into something more suitable." Or: "And—speaking of what's suitable—who wears a satin cloak to a riding party?"

But her mother said nothing. She was piecing together a bodice and sleeve and pretending that all her attention was needed for that, because she always said it was bad business sense to argue with a customer. Only the way her lips were clamped so tightly around the pins she was holding in her mouth gave a hint that she was displeased.

The day was warm, and Georgette felt a trickle of sweat make its way down her back. All that cloth, wasted. All that time, wasted.

"Well," the customer said, "I suppose I'll take the miserable thing off your hands. I have a half-blind maiden aunt who would not be offended by its shortcomings, and I can give it to her to wear in her drafty old house. It will do for keeping drafts off her. But not for the price we discussed, of course. I am *so* peeved that I will not have something new to wear at Lord Randolph's. I'm just taking the cloak so as not to leave you in the lurch. Though I should, since this is not at all what I ordered."

Georgette reached over and tugged the cloak out of the lady's hands. Because it was satin and therefore slippery, and because the lady wasn't expecting Georgette's action, the cloak slid right through the customer's fingers.

"No, really," Georgette said, forcing sweetness into her voice. "One should never settle." She bunched the cloak up and tossed it into the far corner of the little shop, as if to say, "I would not inflict garbage on you." Then she took a pen, leaned over the ledger book, and drew several deep, dark strokes across the line on the lady's account. Without another word, Georgette took out a needle, threaded it, and began to adjust a hem on a dress.

After a long moment, the lady said, "Well!"

Georgette did not look up.

"Well!" the lady repeated. And when Georgette *still* did not look up, the lady stomped out of the shop.

Georgette's mother spat out the pins and said, "That was

not well thought out. *Some* money is better than none."

"Then next time, *you* deal with her," Georgette said. She tossed down the dress and went to fetch the discarded cloak.

Angry and frustrated, Georgette used scissors and a needle to snip open and pick out the seams she had sewed so carefully the night before. She was so upset, she didn't even care when she accidentally stuck the needle deep into her thumb. At least the drop of blood didn't show on the red fabric.

Without a clear plan, once all the old stitches were out, Georgette recut and began to resew.

All afternoon long as Georgette worked, her mother watched. But her mother was too proud a woman to ask, "What are you doing?" This was a good thing, because Georgette wouldn't have had an answer.

She draped the material around a child-sized dress form, the hollow wooden frame that dressmakers use to mark adjustments on an article of clothing, so the customer doesn't have to stand still. (Customers are known for not liking to stand still.) Georgette adjusted the fabric so that it was a full cloak, going all the way around the form, not just over the back and shoulders. She added buttons, and then sewed them closed in the front, with the dress form still inside, holding the cloak in the shape of a little girl. Already Georgette felt a little less angry, a little less sad, a little less lonely. She fashioned a ruffle, which she affixed to the underside of the hem, so that it looked as though the bottom edge of a dress was showing beneath the cloak. She took a pair of leggings and stuffed them, then sewed them beneath the cloak and dress.

By then, it was time to go home, and that's just what Georgette's mother did, leaving Georgette behind. The old woman tarried long enough to say, as she left, "You're wasting good material. That will come out of your portion of what we earn."

Georgette didn't answer. Working by the silvery light of the moon and the flickering light of candles, she took bleached muslin and cut out little gloves, which she attached to the cloak to look like perfectly formed small hands. Late into the night she cut and stitched another piece of muslin, embroidering the features of a sweet little girl's face onto it—the sweet little girl she wished were her own.

When Georgette's mother returned to the shop the following morning, Georgette was asleep, her head resting on her arms on the sewing table. And, sitting in the chair reserved for customers, was a life-sized doll that looked like a girl of 13 years or so.

Georgette awoke when her mother slammed the front door.

"You are a foolish, headstrong thing," her mother said. "No wonder you haven't been able to find a man to be your husband."

Georgette yawned and stretched. "But at least, now, I have a daughter. That makes you a granny."

Her mother made a sour face.

Georgette looked at the doll in the light of morning and found herself more pleased than she'd been the night before. Then, she'd been worried that it was only the dim light and the two previous nights without sleep that made her fabric daughter look so real. But here it was day, and the clothing sewn onto and around the dress form struck Georgette as looking exactly like a person's body, even if the legs—ending in feet wearing the shoes they'd had in the dress shop as a sample from the cobbler—were a bit floppy.

The face, however, went beyond looking exactly like a person's: It was perfect. Delicate eyebrows (with each tiny hair a separate stitch) arched over cerulean blue embroidered eyes—an intense color Georgette thought was much more becoming than her own washed-out hazel eyes. Each eyelash was formed with a thread subtly curled, then stiffened with starch. Georgette had formed the nose with a little bit of extra stuffing beneath the muslin, its shape held by thread she had unwoven from the muslin itself, so that the stitches were invisible. She had used the same technique to fashion the lips, which she had then embroidered over with just the right shade of pink. Lastly, she'd added a blush of color with the powder she had bought once to rouge her own cheeks, but which she had never dared use, because her mother did not approve.

Her mother tugged at the doll's hair, but it was firmly attached to the muslin head.

Probably upset about the wig, Georgette thought. They had

a small assortment in the shop—blonde and auburn and several shades of brown—all on loan from the milliner, so customers could see what a fabric would look like, set off by the different colorings of different people. Georgette had picked the prettiest, and most expensive, golden blonde wig for her creation.

Her mother poked hard at the head of the red-cloaked doll and repeated to Georgette the thought she'd expressed the night before: "Out of *your* share of the wages."

Georgette was barely able to keep from telling her mother to keep her hands to herself.

But when her mother picked up the doll and plunked it down in the space by the window, saying, "Well, I suppose it will do as a sample," Georgette could no longer contain herself.

Georgette rushed forward. "This is not a sample. This is . . ." She held herself up very straight since her creation could not. "This is, as I have said, my daughter."

Now her mother used her bony finger to poke at Georgette's head. "You," she declared, "are obviously moonstruck."

Georgette shrugged, and moved the red cloak-clad figure back to the chair.

All day long, as customers came into the shop, they would coo over what Georgette's mother insisted on calling "the sample." Georgette would smile sweetly and roll her eyes, hoping her expression suggested that the customers should make allowances for her eccentric mother. Two of the ladies were so entranced by the stuffed child's lovely face and beautiful clothes that they asked how much she cost.

"Well," Georgette's mother told them, and she got out a piece of paper, "between the fabric, and the wig, and the work—"

"Mother!" Georgette interrupted. Firmly, she added, "Not for sale."

Georgette's mother sighed. Loudly. She had a strict policy never to argue in front of customers. Though before, this had applied to Georgette, not herself.

As Georgette and her mother were about to close up the shop that evening, one of the women came back. Fingering the fur trim on the red cloak's hood, she said, "I know you told me you weren't selling this, but it would be perfect for my daughter, who will be celebrating her seventh birthday tomorrow. She would be enchanted to own this lifelike doll, even bigger than she is. What's your price?"

Georgette knew the girl, a spoiled brat who would receive a dozen gifts on the morrow, and no doubt drag the bigger-than-herself doll around by the hair, spill things on it, and grow bored with it within the week. "Not for sale," she repeated.

"Hear the lady out," her mother urged. "It's a sample."

"Excuse me," Georgette said. She picked up the *not*-just-a-sample creation, since she knew her mother couldn't be trusted, and left the shop. She considered saying, as though to her "daughter": "Say good-bye to Granny," but refrained, knowing no good could come of that.

People on the street drew closer when they realized she was carrying something made, not born; many smiled and complimented the workmanship. But many also asked, "What's it for?"

What's it for? Georgette fumed. She could well have asked: *What's a child for?*

But she knew her creation was not a real child. A real child could move by itself. And talk. And love Georgette back.

Georgette walked and walked without a specific destination in mind, only to walk off her annoyance, till the streets got less crowded and she came to the edge of the town. The moon was rising over the fields. She watched the-almost-close-enough-to-touch globe and remembered how her mother had called her moonstruck.

That's right, she realized. Tonight was the night of the full moon. It was also midsummer's eve. Midsummer's eve comes but once a year. How often did a full moon happen to fall on that one date? Not every year. Surely not even every dozen years.

It was a rare occurrence.

Perhaps even a magical occurrence.

Georgette was ready for some magic in her life. She walked out of the town, past the fields, and into the woods. The woods were not so very large, because both her town and the next town were growing, and more and more of the trees were being cleared for farmers' fields. But in the woods, there was still a place Georgette had gone to as a child, a spot that the children of the town said was a fairy meadow, where the fairies would dance in the moonlight.

Georgette sat on the grass and waited to see if the children of the town were right.

She woke when a gruff voice said: "Ay! What's all this then?"

She rubbed the sleep out of her eyes and saw it was morning, and a man was leaning over her.

He looked as gruff as he sounded, and he was holding an ax, which was alarming. But there was a cart on the path that skirted the edge of the small clearing, a cart overflowing with branches and chunks of tree trunks. He was a woodcutter, which gave him a reason to be in the woods with a blade; and that set Georgette's mind somewhat at ease.

"Oh, you're alive, are you?" the woodcutter said. "Well, I suppose that's good. Though where your sense has gone, sleeping in the woods, I don't know. Too much to drink, I'm guessing. Too much celebrating midsummer's eve."

Georgette didn't think she should argue with him. She didn't think she should try to explain. What *had* she been thinking? Too much work, and not enough sleep. What had she hoped to gain by bringing that doll out here? In fact, what had she hoped to gain by making it in the first place?

She would pick the thing up and take it home. She'd tell her mother that yes, of course, it should be set in the window as a sample of their craftsmanship.

Except that . . .

She looked around, trying to remember where she had set down the doll.

Except that . . .

Had she rolled over onto it? No.

She hadn't put it someplace, then continued to walk, had she? She hadn't been that befuddled by being overtired and upset with the world in general and her mother in particular. Had she?

She looked at the woodcutter. "Have you seen . . . ? Did you take . . . ?"

But that didn't make any sense. First, he didn't look like the sort of man who would be interested in a doll. Second, where would he have put it—hidden in his cart, under all that wood? But, if he'd wanted it, he wouldn't have needed to hide it. All he'd have had to do was take it and continue on his way rather than waking her.

Had someone else done precisely that? Come upon her while she slept, stolen the doll, then continued down the path? If so, she was fortunate her throat hadn't been slit in the bargain.

Though her mother would surely have a great deal to say about *that*.

The woodcutter said, "Seen what? Taken what? You asking about that little red riding hood girl?"

Men never did understand fashion. Georgette was about to point out that it was a full cloak, not a simple riding hood, but then she realized what he'd said. She sucked in her breath. She refused to acknowledge the hope that fluttered like a butterfly in her heart. She told herself: *He has seen the doll.* "Where?" she demanded.

"Over yonder," the woodcutter said. "Beyond that bend. Gathering flowers."

Even someone who did not dare believe could not find a reasonable explanation for that.

Georgette ran in the direction the woodcutter had pointed.

Just after the spot where the path curved, someone was bending over, picking wildflowers. Someone wearing the red cloak. That someone looked up, and Georgette recognized the cerulean blue eyes.

"Hello," Georgette said breathlessly, from the running, from the wish that had brought her to the fairy meadow—the wish she had not put into words, but that had come true.

"Hello," the girl in the red cloak said.

As long as wishes were coming true, Georgette could have wished that her new daughter might have sounded warmer and more friendly, that she might have thrown her arms around Georgette and cried, "Mother!"

But she's hollow on the inside, Georgette remembered, thinking of the dressmaker's form that was her daughter's ribcage and spine. *I never put in a heart.*

She had no sooner thought that, when three young farmer boys came riding their farm horses down the path, talking about the midsummer eve festivities in the town the night before, and how their fathers were going to tan them for staying out all night.

The girl in the red cloak turned toward them and gave a dazzling smile.

I never gave her teeth, Georgette thought peevishly. But the smile must have come from the fairies, along with the ability to wake up alive, and to wander away from the person next to her when she awoke, and to go off on her own picking flowers, and to say "hello" in such a cool, bored voice to the mother who had wished her into existence.

"Whoa-ho!" one of the young men said, seeing the beautiful girl. All three boys pulled their mounts to a stop.

Another of the boys gave a long, low wolf whistle.

The third, being the most articulate, said, "Hey there, beautiful."

Just as Georgette was about to say, "That's no way to talk to my daughter," her daughter winked and said, "Hey there, handsome."

"Care to give us a kiss?" the boy asked.

"Now see here . . ." Georgette protested.

The girl in the red cloak put her hand on her hip and said, "Either you've got to come down, or I've got to go."

The boys scrambled off their horses and formed a line. Georgette was too surprised to do more than stare as the daughter she had wished so hard for gave each of the boys a kiss. "My, what big eyes you have," she cooed to the first. "My, what strong arms you have," she said to the second. "My, what firm lips you have," she told the third.

The boy who had whistled, no doubt emboldened by the girl's kiss or the compliment he received, asked, "Wanna ride?"

"She does not," Georgette told him.

"Yes, I do," her daughter said enthusiastically.

That's what I get for stuffing her empty head with muslin, Georgette thought as the boys scuffled with one another, each vying to be the one to get the beautiful girl up onto his horse.

Whistler-boy finally won.

There was no fighting what had to be. "Good-bye," Georgette called after them.

The girl had hiked up her cloak so that it looked almost as short as a little red riding hood. She never looked back as they rode away.

Perhaps Mother was right about children being too much trouble, Georgette thought as she began walking back toward town, alone once again.

   She would have to see about getting herself a cat.

Little Red Riding Hood's Family

Once upon a time, long after people had found out that their families could sometimes be an embarrassment, but before there were advice columnists you could complain to, there was a girl named Roselle. She was an only child, so there were no siblings to humiliate her, but her parents seemed determined to make up for that lack. Despite being old—obviously they were old enough to be her parents—they acted like lovesick young people.

One day in their little cottage in the woods, Roselle's parents were acting particularly silly. Roselle was clearing things off the supper table. Father had just brought in a bucketful of water from the well to heat on the fire for Mother to wash the dishes. Suddenly, and for no apparent reason other than boredom, or maybe because Father was singing an annoying nursery-rhyme song, Mother scooped a handful of sudsy water and tossed it at Father.

"Tag! You're it!" she cried. But as she turned to run, she

slipped in the water she'd dripped. Down she went, though not before grabbing at the table to try to steady herself, so down also came the tablecloth, used dishes, and leftover food.

Roselle and Father came rushing to her side.

"Ouch!" Mother cried, rubbing her ankle. "Oh, I feel like such a fool."

Roselle loved her parents too much to say *As well you should*. But she couldn't help thinking it. They *had* been acting like children. Again.

"I think it's just twisted," Mother told them. "I'll be all right in a moment." But when she tried to stand, she couldn't put weight on her foot.

Father asked Roselle, "Is there anything you can do?" which was just like him. He seemed to think her talents were unlimited.

But Roselle shook her head. She didn't know much about the healing arts. "Raise her foot?" she suggested. But it was only a guess.

Father carried Mother to a chair and fetched a stool on which to rest her foot.

"Better?" he asked.

"Yes," Mother assured them. "I just need to catch my breath, then I'll be as good as new. It's just . . ."

Roselle saw her mother's gaze land on the basket she had prepared—supper for Mother's mother, Granny. Mother had planned on taking it over that evening.

"Oh," Roselle said, knowing what Mother was thinking, "I

don't think you should be walking right away." It didn't take exceptional healing arts to see that Mother wouldn't be able to get to the other end of the small house, much less through the woods.

Father said, "It's not as though Granny is sick or incapacitated or has no food in the house. She can make do this one evening." Father and Granny weren't on the best terms.

Mother shook her head. "But I told her this morning after market that I would be over later today. She won't have prepared anything. And if I don't go there, she'll be worried and she'll come here."

Father gulped. Everyone knew he was a bit afraid of Granny.

And Granny didn't tend to help matters. She liked to say, "All the best mothers-in-law are scary."

"I'll go," Roselle offered.

Father said, "But it will be getting dark soon." He sighed. "I'll go." He said it like a man volunteering to walk into a den of wolves.

Behind his back, Roselle rolled her eyes.

Mother laughed at the idea of Father facing Granny on his own. They all knew he tried to avoid her when she had what he would call "her moods." Mother said, "It's not as if the woods are dangerous. And you know Roselle can take care of herself."

Roselle could see Father weighing this in his head.

Mother added, "And Roselle doesn't let Granny intimidate her. They're like two peas in a pod."

"They are *not*," Father said indignantly.

In fact, Granny could be just as embarrassing, in her own way, as Mother and Father. Roselle leaned in quickly and kissed Father's cheek. "I'll be back before you have time to clean up the mess you've made."

"Ah," Father said, "so now we know your real reason for offering to go." But he was laughing and obviously relieved.

Roselle kissed Mother, too, then threw her favorite little hooded capelet over her shoulders against the evening chill. Snatching up the basket, she called, "Take care!" to her parents.

The late afternoon sun had sunk below the trees, so the woods were getting a bit gloomy. But the moon was already showing big and full, pale and low in the sky. Before the sun was gone entirely, the moon would be high and bright enough to light the path.

There was no reason to hurry, and Roselle had the opportunity to look for high mallow. Not only was it pretty with its purplish pink flowers, but it was good for the digestion—something Granny could use, for she sometimes gulped down her food in a way that ailed her stomach—not to mention that indigestion made her noisy and awkward in polite company.

But the flowers weren't so easy to find, and after a while Roselle heard an owl hoot, and she was aware that the time had gotten away from her.

As Mother had said, Roselle *did* feel perfectly capable of taking care of herself. But for some reason—perhaps because of the shifting shadows as clouds drifted across the luminous moon, perhaps from having seen how quickly her family had gone from fun and laughter to her mother getting hurt, perhaps from hearing the rustling in the underbrush as some small animal dove for cover as if mistaking her for that owl—for whatever reason, Roselle found herself just the slightest bit uneasy as she now hurried on her way.

Almost, she thought, as if some sixth sense were warning that someone was watching her.

But that was silly.

What danger could there be going to Granny's house, a short trip she had been making by herself since she'd been a small child?

Though not—ever before—past sunset.

When Roselle arrived at Granny's doorstep, she saw the glow of candlelight beneath the door.

Relieved to be there, Roselle knocked.

And knocked again.

And again.

"Granny!" she called.

She remembered the feeling of being watched, and was aware—as she had rarely been before—how far away Granny's house actually was from any neighbors.

"Granny!" she called again, louder. And when there was still no answer, she opened the door to peek in.

Not a sign of Granny.

The place was neat, as Granny always kept it, with the pillows fluffed on the chairs, and an arrangement of wildflowers on the kitchen table—including high mallow—which meant there had been no need for Roselle's tarrying to search out some of her own. A pretty placemat Granny, herself, had woven was also on the table, and arranged on this was a wooden bowl and mug and a spoon. Usually when Roselle came to visit, Granny's house smelled deliciously of soup or stew simmering on the fire, or of fresh-baked bread, or of a steaming tart made from berries Granny had picked from her garden. But Mother had told Granny this morning that she would send over dinner, so Roselle could smell only the flowers—no food.

Roselle pushed the door farther open, hoping to find Granny in the far corner at her spinning wheel, hoping to hear Granny call out, "Come on in and close the door behind you before you invite all the nighttime creatures in."

But of course Granny didn't call out. If Granny had been there, then Roselle would have heard the *whirr, whirr* of the wheel.

Hesitating in the doorway, half inside the house and half outside, Roselle saw the spinning wheel standing idle amidst piles of wool ready to be drawn into yarn. The other door, the one to Granny's bedroom, was slightly ajar—and from the bedroom came a noise.

Thud!

Not so very loud, but distinct.

Like something dropped, Roselle thought. Except that a moment later, the sound repeated. Or another sound very like the first. Then a third time. And a fourth. There was a low whine, like an animal in distress.

Roselle tiptoed the rest of the way into the living room, not sure what she was afraid of seeing.

In her agitation at not finding Granny, in her hurry to determine there was nothing wrong going on in the other room, in her anxiety to move silently (in case this was a situation needing stealth)—with all of that going on, Roselle forgot the being-watched feeling she'd had in the woods, and she didn't close the front door behind her.

She set the dinner-and-flower-packed basket down on the floor, so she could move fast, her hands unencumbered. Granny might sometimes be an embarrassment, but she *was* Granny. And if she were in trouble, Roselle would do her best to help. She took a deep breath. Then she dashed to the bedroom doorway, careful to avoid the floorboard that creaked, so as not to warn any intruder—if there was one—about her arrival.

At first she didn't see Granny in the bedroom. She wasn't in the bed or at the dressing table.

Then Roselle heard another *clunk*, and out of the corner of her eye, she caught a movement.

And there was Granny, kneeling on the floor, half inside the closet, surrounded by shoes and boots and slippers. Evidently she was looking for something, and tossing over her shoulder those things that were not what she was looking for.

Roselle rapped her knuckles against the door frame so as

not to startle Granny.

It's a very bad thing to startle an old granny.

Particularly an old granny who's a werewolf.

Most particularly an old granny who's in her were-wolf form.

"My, Granny," Roselle called out to let Granny know she was there, "what big, furry ears you have! I would have thought you'd have heard me come in."

Granny turned around. "Roselle!" she said. Her voice was always kind of barky when it came out of her wolf muzzle instead of her human mouth. "There you are! I was beginning to worry. I was just about to change out of this old nightdress and go over to your house to make sure everything was all right. But I couldn't find four matching shoes."

Granny was not the kind of person who would ever leave the house without being properly dressed. Some werewolves, of course, went without clothes when the change came upon them. But Granny always said, "Nobody with any kind of manners would leave the house naked except for a fur coat, and I'm certainly not going to do that just because the moon is full and I've gone from biped to quadruped."

Roselle thought linen and lace didn't go well with fur, and she found Granny's fashion sense mortifyingly old-fashioned.

But Roselle still thought Granny was a sweetheart. She was wearing her nightdress, which was roomy enough to accommodate her with or without a tail, and she had three skinny boots on, with her left front paw bare.

Roselle said, "Mother twisted her ankle. She's fine, but I thought I'd better bring the basket she prepared for you."

"Oh, that's so kind," Granny said. "It *is* difficult to peel vegetables when one has four feet and no hands."

Roselle leaned over her to look in the closet. "Is that the other boot?" she asked. "On the shelf, behind the hatbox?"

"How did it ever get up there?" Granny asked. She might have been fastidious about how she dressed, but not about her closet. Now that she didn't have to leave the house, she took off the three boots she *had* found and tossed them aside. "So," she said, slamming the closet door before anything could fall back out. She licked her lips. "What treats did your mother prepare for me?"

Before Roselle could answer, the floorboard behind them creaked, a sudden reminder of that being-watched sensation, and that she had left the front door wide open.

Roselle whirled around and found a man standing there, tall and thin and impossibly pale, his skin almost as white as his teeth, which gleamed in the candlelight.

"Oh, no," he said as soon as his red eyes lit on Granny. "Not a werewolf. I hate furry necks."

Granny threw her paws up in the air. "Oh, no," she echoed, "not another vampire. This is the third vampire this year. What's this town coming to?"

The vampire looked beyond Granny to Roselle. He raised

his arms, his cape spreading out behind him like great bat wings as he took a step forward, saying, "However, *you*, my tender little morsel . . ."

But before he could get any farther, Roselle uttered a magic spell and transformed him into a frog—a pale, sickly-looking frog. Out of the cottage he hopped, as fast as his little frog legs would let him.

"Ewww," Granny said. "One less vampire, but now the woods will have a blood-sucking frog."

"Sorry," Roselle said. "I didn't think. I know witches have a reputation for turning *princes* into frogs, but I figured: What are my chances of ever running into a prince?"

Granny shrugged. "Good point," she said. "I was always sorry that the magic skipped your mother. But you, my dear, make a fine witch."

Arm in paw, they walked into the living room to get the basket of goodies, and to close the door against any other visitors.

Granny and the Wolf

Once upon a time, before online dating services, there was a granny who had an unwelcome suitor.

Nelda might well have been the youngest widowed granny in the village of Farnsworth, and she was certainly considered one of the most attractive, but about one thing there was absolutely no doubt: she was definitely the richest. Nelda was also smart—smart enough to know it was her wealth that made Gladwyn the woodcutter so interested in her.

"Nelda," he'd say to her on every occasion he could, "your husband has been dead three years now. It's time to get over him. A woman such as your fine self should not be alone." Then he would wink at her and nudge her with his elbow if she wasn't quick enough to avoid it.

Now, Gladwyn himself was considered a fine catch by many of the older women in Farnsworth, since he had thick curly hair, much of it still dark, and he still had all his teeth.

But although Nelda admired good dental appearance as much as anyone else, she couldn't help but compare Gladwyn to her own dear Roderick. She remembered how Roderick had valued her for other things than youth, good looks, or her hardworking and thrifty ways that had resulted in the couple having enough money to put aside for a rainy day. Roderick had praised Nelda for her kind heart, for the way she was gentle with everyone's feelings, and for her concern for others' well-being. And those were all traits she had valued in Roderick, too, traits which Gladwyn was noticeably lacking. Gladwyn was full of himself, and he had a mean streak that those who were overly preoccupied with his full set of teeth were willing to overlook.

If Gladwyn heard of Nelda giving something away to someone who needed it more than she did, he would say, "Nelda, you are too generous to those less deserving than your fine self." If Nelda bought or made something for her son, Frick, or his wife, Aurelia, or her granddaughter, Scarlet, Gladwyn would say: "Nelda, not to criticize your fine self, but you are spoiling them." Gladwyn liked to warn Nelda that people were taking advantage of her fine self, by which she took him to mean she was spending the money he hoped would be his if he could talk her into marrying him.

Nelda did not feel Gladwyn should be the rainy day she and Roderick had saved up for.

One brisk autumn afternoon when Nelda was on her way to the market to sell her homemade tarts, she saw Gladwyn in the village street ahead of her. She was too kind a person to just come out and say: *Don't even talk to me, you greedy, boring, self-centered man.* But the thought of his nudges to her ribs or of one more "your fine self" drove her to duck between two houses to avoid him. Then, overwhelmed by the desire not to see him, she hurried into the woods to take the shortcut back home.

As she walked down the path enjoying the smell of the fallen leaves, she heard a whimpering noise as though someone were in pain. "Hello?" Nelda called.

The noise stopped, but no one answered, which was strange since someone seemed to be in trouble. A moment later, the whimpering resumed, quieter, as though whoever it was didn't want to be heard, but couldn't help it.

Nelda stepped off the path and followed the sound. The crisp leaves beneath her feet crackled, and whoever was crying must once again have caught his or her breath. "It's all right," Nelda said. "I only want to help."

Still, whoever it wasn't didn't call out, "I'm here." Or even: "I'm fine—mind your own business and leave me alone."

Nelda climbed a little rise, and there before her was the one who was in trouble.

But it wasn't a man, woman, or child: It was a wolf. And its back right leg was caught in a trap.

"Oh, you poor thing," Nelda said. Nelda would have felt

sorry for any creature in pain. But doubly so for this poor wolf, because Nelda knew that Gladwyn was the only woodsman who set traps so close to the village. It might as easily have been a child caught so cruelly. It might as easily have been herself.

The wolf looked at her, with eyes bright with pain and fear.

Nelda knew an injured animal could be dangerous: it could lash out. But she suspected that Gladwyn would—if he could— set a trap for her, and that made her feel a certain kinship with this beautiful, wild animal.

She put down the basket of apple tarts she had hoped to sell in Farnsworth and said in a calm voice, "I won't hurt you. You're safe now. Everything will be fine."

The wolf, a small young female, ducked her head but continued to watch as Nelda slowly approached.

"There," Nelda said softly, and reached out her hand for the wolf to sniff. "See, I'm a friend." She stood far enough back so that if the wolf looked ready to bite, she could snatch her hand away. "Do I smell friendly?" she crooned. "I hope so. Yes. Yes, I *am* friendly. Yes, I'm going to help you."

When the wolf seemed ready for it, Nelda set her hand gently on the creature's chest, then worked her way up to scratch her under the chin. The wolf closed her eyes, obviously enjoying the scratching.

"Such a fine girl you are," Nelda told her. "Yes, you are.

You know you can trust me, don't you? Now, don't get excited: I'm going to move. I'm going to see about getting that nasty trap to let go of your leg."

Slowly, Nelda crouched down in front of the wolf.

The wolf opened her eyes and watched.

"You're doing fine," Nelda told her. She bent over the trap. Working against the spring that strained to hold it shut, she pried the trap's jaws open, being careful not to cut herself on the metal teeth.

The wolf stepped out of the trap, and Nelda breathed a sigh of relief that the creature's leg apparently wasn't broken, although it bore vicious gashes from where the wolf had tried to pull free before Nelda had arrived.

Still mindful of her own hands, Nelda let the trap snap shut on empty air.

"There," she said, somewhat surprised that the wolf had not run off immediately.

Like a big, friendly dog, the wolf licked the back of Nelda's hand.

"Oh, you sweetie," Nelda said to her. "You're welcome." She got up, briefly resting her hand on the wolf's shoulder, and still the wolf did not run away. Nelda went back to where she'd left the basket of apple tarts and lifted the cloth that covered them. "May I bind this around your leg to stop the bleeding?"

Of course, the wolf didn't answer, but neither did she run away, so Nelda fastened the cloth over the wounds.

"If you come home with me," Nelda said, not that she

really thought the wolf could understand her, "I can put some salve on those cuts." She picked up the trap, intending to put it into her basket so no other unfortunate animal could be ensnared. However, the apple tarts took up too much room for the trap to fit, so Nelda took out one of the tarts and put it on the ground.

The wolf came over and ate it.

Whether it was because of Nelda's words or the apple tart, the wolf followed Nelda home, though limping slowly. Periodically, Nelda would pause to let her rest and to give her another apple tart.

Finally, with only three tarts to spare, they arrived home.

"You stay here," Nelda told the wolf on her doorstep. "I'll bring the salve out."

But the wolf, having followed her this far, followed Nelda into the house.

Oh, well, Nelda thought. She put the basket on the kitchen table and got the salve out of the cupboard. "This may sting at first," she warned, but the wolf didn't flinch. After Nelda had once again bound up the wolf's leg, the animal lay down on the floor by the kitchen hearth, apparently ready to make herself at home.

"Well, I suppose that's fine for a little bit," Nelda said.

But in another moment, there was a knocking at her door.

The wolf raised her head from her front paws but didn't make a sound.

"Who is it?" Nelda asked.

"It's me, Granny," came the sweet voice of her only grandchild, Scarlet, the daughter of Nelda's son Frick. Normally, the sound of Scarlet's voice would fill Nelda with happy anticipation. But Frick was a bit of a worrywart. No, Frick was a *great deal* of a worrywart. Ever since Roderick had died, Frick had been encouraging Nelda to move into town with him—"So Aurelia, Scarlet, and I can take care of you," he said. Nelda loved her son's family, but she didn't believe she needed taking care of. And if Frick learned that she was keeping a wolf in the house . . . She could just imagine Frick, an excitable man in the best of circumstances, getting hysterical at what he would see as the danger.

"Um, wait a moment," Nelda called out to Scarlet.

She put her hands on her hips and looked at the wolf. "What am I going to do with you?" she whispered.

The wolf cocked her head, as though trying to help Nelda think.

Nelda glanced around the kitchen. Perhaps if the wolf sat under the table . . . but none of Nelda's tablecloths reached down to the floor. Nelda briefly considered draping the table with a sheet, but Scarlet, a bright and inquisitive child, would surely notice and ask Nelda why she was using bed linens to cover the table.

The kitchen was useless for hiding. The parlor? Perhaps she could put the wolf behind the big chair that used to be Roderick's. If Nelda told Scarlet she couldn't enter the parlor but must sit in the kitchen, and if the wolf didn't move a muscle the entire length of Scarlet's visit . . .

But surely Scarlet would ask *why* she couldn't go into the parlor. That left the bedroom. Nelda motioned for the wolf to follow her. Obediently, the wolf did, though Nelda winced at the sound of wolf toenails on the wooden floor. "Quiet," she warned.

She was convinced the wolf did her best to walk on tiptoe.

"Sit," Nelda commanded, as firmly as someone can command in a whisper.

The wolf sat on the little rug by Nelda's bed.

Since that had worked surprisingly well, Nelda added, "Stay. And keep quiet."

Nelda backed out of the room and closed the door as the wolf stayed behind and kept quiet.

Nelda could hear Scarlet tapping on the front door again. "Granny," her granddaughter called impatiently.

Nelda wiped her hands on the skirt of her dress and walked across the kitchen to open the door. "Scarlet!" she said. "Such a pleasant surprise." Maybe, she hoped, Scarlet was going someplace else and had dropped by simply to say *hello*. Although normally Nelda loved Scarlet's visits, now she stood blocking the doorway, since keeping Scarlet outside was the surest way to prevent her from learning that her grandmother had a wolf for a houseguest. Why couldn't Scarlet be like other twelve-year-olds, Nelda wondered for the first time ever, and not tell her parents everything?

"May I come in?" Scarlet asked.

"Mmmm . . ." Nelda toyed with the idea of saying *no*. But that would result in questions. "Mmmm, yes. Of course. Certainly." She still hesitated; but now, invited, Scarlet kissed Nelda's cheek and walked past her into the kitchen.

"It's good to see you, Granny."

"It's good to see you, Scarlet."

"What's that I smell?"

Nelda sniffed. Could her granddaughter smell the wolf? Nelda hadn't noticed that the wolf had an odor. "Mmmm . . . apple tarts?"

"No," Scarlet said. She looked around the room as if hoping for a hint. "It's . . . it's like that salve you put on my knees when I fell down collecting acorns."

"Oh," Nelda said, relieved. "Yes, the salve."

"You didn't hurt yourself, did you?"

She couldn't say yes. Frick had this fear that his mother would fall down in her house and that nobody would know about it for days. If Scarlet went home with a story that Nelda had somehow injured herself, Frick would be on her doorstep before the afternoon was over. She said, "Once in a while I put some on my hands to keep my fingers limber." Then she added, "Probably best not to say anything to your father. You know how he worries."

Scarlet nodded, although Nelda knew the child could be a

worrier, too. Then Scarlet said, "Actually . . ."

"What?"

"I'd rather not tell them I was here. Mother and Father said not to keep bothering you. . . ."

With her mind still distracted by the wolf, Nelda needed a moment to realize what Scarlet was talking about. "The dress!" she said. Scarlet was twelve this year, finally old enough to attend the harvest festival dance next week, and Nelda had promised to make her a dress. She was taking apart an old gown of her own—too fancy and too out-of-date for anything she did these days—and she was remaking it in a smaller size and in a more up-to-date fashion. "It's coming along well," Nelda said. "We're almost ready for a fitting."

Scarlet was so excited, she couldn't stand still. "Yes, please," she said, apparently missing the word *almost*. "I can't wait to see it."

"Mmmm . . ." Nelda said, for the dress was hanging in her wardrobe in the bedroom. But she couldn't say *no* to the expectant look on her granddaughter's face. "Wait here," she told Scarlet, then offered as an excuse: "The bedroom is a bit messy." She sat Scarlet down in Roderick's chair, then gave it a twist to get it, and Scarlet, positioned facing away from the bedroom door.

As Nelda went to get the dress, she glanced back and saw that Scarlet was watching her. Nelda pointed out the window. "Is that my neighbor's cow loose again?"

When Scarlet turned around to look, Nelda opened the

bedroom door, stepped in, then closed the door behind her.

The wolf was sitting obediently where Nelda had left her.

"You are *such* a good girl," Nelda whispered to her. She opened the wardrobe and reached in for the dress.

Scarlet tapped on the bedroom door. "No cow out there, Granny. Shouldn't I come in to try on the dress, since that's where the mirror is?"

"Mmmm . . ." Nelda answered. "Good point."

The doorknob rattled.

"But *wait!*" Nelda threw herself against the door so that Scarlet couldn't push it open. She pointed at the wolf, then pointed at the wardrobe.

The wolf cocked her head at Nelda.

Nelda repeated the motion more emphatically.

The wolf climbed into the wardrobe.

"Good girl," Nelda whispered. "Don't be frightened." Wolves couldn't be frightened of the dark, could they? A lot of times they came out at night. But her wolf might be frightened about the closed-in space. Nelda hoped not. "Lie down." Very gently, she closed the wardrobe door. Then she opened the bedroom door.

"There you are!" she said to Scarlet, quite loudly, to cover the sound of the wolf lying down in the wardrobe.

Scarlet looked a bit startled at her grandmother's energetic greeting, considering they had seen each other only moments ago. Then she glanced around the bedroom. "This isn't messy," Scarlet said. "You haven't seen messy until you've seen my room."

"Oh, well," Nelda said.

But it wasn't the state of the room that Scarlet was interested in. "Oh!" she cried, reaching for the dress her grandmother was still holding. "It's beautiful!"

"Careful of the pins."

Scarlet ran her hands over the rich red fabric. "This is the most beautiful dress, ever."

"Do you want to try it on?"

Scarlet was already reaching to untie the sash of the dress she was wearing. She let the dress fall to the floor, where she kicked it out of the way, a telltale sign that she hadn't been exaggerating to call her room at home messy. She held her arms up over her head, and Nelda, being mindful of the pins, helped her granddaughter get into the new red dress.

Scarlet turned herself this way and that in front of the mirror. "Oh, Granny! I love it!"

Nelda said, "You'll be the prettiest girl at the dance, no matter what you wear. But this *does* suit you. Let me just make some adjustments. . . ." She moved some of the pins.

Inside the wardrobe, the wolf must have shifted position.

"Granny, what's that noise?"

"Mice," Nelda said. "That's why I didn't want you to come in. Me, I don't mind them. I think they're cute." She raised her voice for the wolf to hear. "It's all right for you to be in there, little sweetie, but you need to keep quiet now."

"I'm not afraid of mice," Scarlet said. "But that one sounds big."

"Mice always plump up in the autumn to get themselves ready for the winter."

There was a bigger noise, this time from the front of the house.

Scarlet said, "Do the really big mice knock to get in?"

Although it was rude to just call out instead of going to the front door, Nelda raised her voice to ask, "Who's there?"

Gladwyn's voice announced, "It's me, Gladwyn." His tone indicated that of course this would be welcome news.

"Drat!" Nelda whispered. "I don't want to see him!"

"Too late to pretend you're not home," Scarlet pointed out. "What's wrong with Gladwyn?"

Nelda looked at her beloved granddaughter and said, "For one thing, he thinks I spoil you. He says I shouldn't give you so much. If he sees you in this dress, I won't hear the end of it for weeks."

"Well," Scarlet said, "that's . . . just wrong. But, if you want, I can hide here in the bedroom until he leaves."

Another wolf-shifting-herself sound came from the wardrobe. How long could the poor creature be expected to stay in there, with no idea why?

"Mice," Nelda reminded Scarlet. "I have a better idea." Recalling that underneath the kitchen table might be a good hiding place—with a long-enough tablecloth—she whipped the sheet off the bed. A man was unlikely to be able to tell the difference between bed linens and table linens.

She led Scarlet out of the bedroom, shutting the door behind them to drown out any more noises the wolf might make. Then she motioned for Scarlet to crawl beneath the table.

From outside, Gladwyn's voice called, "Nelda my sweet, are you there?"

Nelda bit her lip to keep from answering: *I am NOT your sweet. And, no, I am not here.*

But she suspected Gladwyn was so full of himself that such a response would convince him something had to be wrong, and then she'd never get him to leave. So, instead, she called, "I'll be there momentarily." She flung the sheet over the table, covering table and basket alike with the remaining apple tarts, and she warned Scarlet, just as she had the wolf, "Keep quiet and keep still." Then she went to the door.

"Gladwyn," she said, standing firmly in the doorway to block his view.

"Nelda," he said, "is anything amiss with your fine self?"

So much for trying to forestall that question.

"No," she told him. "Why do you ask?"

"It's been several days since I've seen you in the village, and I started to worry about you, all alone in this house out in the woods. It's not safe, you know, for a woman such as your fine self to be all alone. Your husband has been dead for three years now. It's time you got yourself a new man to protect you from evil or mishap." He winked at her, but fortunately there was no way for him to nudge her in the side with his elbow, since he was standing in front of her.

Nelda could have told him that he hadn't seen her in the village this last week because she had grown especially diligent at avoiding him. She could have told him that a husband should be for more than protection. She could have told him that, in any case, *he* was the only evil or mishap from which she was in need of protection.

But while she was trying to figure out what she should say, a soft but distinct noise came from inside the house—a dejected, warble-like whine.

"What was that?" Gladwyn asked.

"What?" Nelda said. She cleared her throat, hoping he might think the noise had come from her rather than from a lonely wolf who felt abandoned in a wardrobe. Nelda coughed. She cleared her throat again. Had her caller been her son, Frick, rather than her suitor, Gladwyn, all these sounds of congestion would have convinced him that she had caught some dread contagion.

Gladwyn knew the noise hadn't come from her. He tried to see around her. "I heard something," he said.

"Mice," Nelda told him, weaving, to keep her head in his way.

The whine repeated, a little less quiet, a little more definite.

"Unhappy mice," Nelda amended.

The warble quality diminished; the whine escalated.

Gladwyn looked ready to push right past her. "There's something terribly awry in your home," he insisted. "Let me in, and I'll deal with it."

"Oh," Nelda said. "*That* noise. That's . . . my granddaughter."

"Your granddaughter?" Gladwyn echoed. "What ails the child?"

The wolf in the wardrobe howled.

"Stomach ache," Nelda said. "I really should see to her." She took a step back so as to close the door, but Gladwyn stepped right into the kitchen.

Nelda hastily glanced at the table to make sure Scarlet was still hidden underneath and that the tablecloth sheet reached all the way to the floor.

Gladwyn said, "If she needs to be carried to the apothecary, a man like myself could do that more readily than a woman alone, without a man to take care of her."

"No," Nelda assured him. "It's—"

The wolf howled again. Nelda could hear her scratching at the wardrobe door. Nelda finished, "It's nothing for which she needs a physician's care."

Gladwyn took a step toward the bedroom. "Better safe than sorry," he said.

"Stop!" Nelda commanded.

Gladwyn hesitated, but Nelda knew he could not be

diverted entirely. She said, "Let me make sure she's properly dressed. She would be very distressed otherwise." Though it made her cringe inwardly to say it, she knew how to play up to Gladwyn's notion of womankind. She added, "You know how silly we females can be about such things."

Gladwyn smiled indulgently.

"Just . . ."–Nelda held up a finger– ". . . stay right here. *Right. Here.*"

As she circled around the kitchen table, she saw that Scarlet had raised one edge of the sheet to peek out toward the bedroom. From where he currently stood, Gladwyn wouldn't be able to see, but Nelda took the time to go to the table as though one of the wrinkles was too much to bear a moment longer, even with a sick grandchild in the other room.

Scarlet whispered, "So who's this other granddaughter I've never heard of, the one with the bad stomach?"

Nelda pulled the bit of sheet out of Scarlet's hand so that it once more reached the floor. From between clenched teeth she whispered, "If you want me to finish making that dress, keep out of sight."

Before she returned to the bedroom, she looked back at Gladwyn to make sure he was still where he was supposed to be.

Obviously thinking of himself as her savior, he gave a self-satisfied smile.

Nelda pushed open the door, then rapidly shut it behind her, leaning against it. At the moment, what she most wanted was to put a chair in front of the door, blocking it, and never open it again; but she knew that wouldn't work for more than a few moments. Gladwyn would break in if he had to, in order to prove himself helpful.

She flung open the wardrobe, and the wolf leapt out, then sat down on the rug, happy once more and waiting to see what would come next.

Nelda glanced at the window, but estimated it was too high up for a wolf with an injured back leg to get up to and out of. Instead she patted the bed. "Here, girl," she said.

Obediently, the wolf jumped onto the bed.

This would never work. Still, Nelda reached under the pillow and got her hair bonnet, which she placed on the wolf's head, tying it under the animal's chin. The wolf—Nelda was sure of it—looked embarrassed.

But when Nelda commanded, "Lie down," the wolf did, resting her head on her paws.

"No, you should be going this way." Obviously, there was no explaining to a wolf the difference between a headboard and a footboard. "Oh, never mind." Nelda knew she should consider herself lucky the wolf hadn't ended up sideways across the bed. Nelda moved the pillow to the other end of the bed and drew the comforter up over the wolf's body. "Good girl," she said. "Stay." She arranged the comforter to cover the wolf's front paws, but had it dip down in the middle, revealing the back of the wolf's bonnet-covered head, because surely

Gladwyn would be suspicious if the comforter covered Nelda's "granddaughter" entirely.

Before Nelda could step away from the bed, Gladwyn was opening the door. "Are you ready for me to carry the poor youngster to the apothecary?" he asked.

In a whisper so soft that Nelda couldn't even be sure the wolf could hear, she repeated, "Stay," and hoped the wolf knew that meant both *Don't get out of bed* and *Don't turn your head.* She herself stayed by the bed, her hand resting on the wolf's shoulder.

To Gladwyn she said, "No, the worst seems to be over. She's resting comfortably now. Thank you so much for your kind offer. We should just leave and let her sleep now."

Clearly disappointed, Gladwyn said, "But surely to be safe—" He interrupted himself by sucking in a shocked breath. "Nelda," he gasped, gaping at the figure in the bed, "what a skinny, hairy leg your granddaughter has!"

Nelda quickly twitched the comforter to cover the wolf's exposed knee. "That's a very personal remark," she told him. "As a matter of fact, all the women in my family have an abundance of hair on our limbs. In truth, I need to take a razor to my arms and legs every day. Actually, to be perfectly honest, that is one of the things I most miss Roderick for: Being able to reach those pesky patches of hair on my back. So you're right, there are certain things I can't do for myself." She gave him an extra-bright smile.

While Gladwyn was busy digesting that thought, there was a knock on the front door, followed by the sound of Frick's voice calling out, "Mother?"

There were days that *nobody* came to call. Why was everyone here today?

Nelda's breath escaped in a hiss. She whispered at Gladwyn, "My son can't find you in my bedroom! What would he say?"

"Well, explain that the little one has been feeling poorly—"

"No!" Nelda interrupted, for Frick would never mistake a wolf—with or without a bonnet and comforter—for his daughter. Thinking quickly, she explained, "Don't forget, my poor dead husband was his father. Frick would go into an absolute *rage* to find you here."

Incredulously, Gladwyn asked, "Frick would?" for Frick was not the type of man who had a violent temper. But Nelda was nodding so emphatically that Gladwyn said, "Maybe you can distract him at the door, and I'll hide under the kitchen table."

"No!" Nelda said. "Get in the wardrobe."

She shoved Gladwyn into the wardrobe before he could protest. "It smells kind of musty in here," he said, sniffing loudly.

"Mice!" Nelda assured him and slammed the door shut.

The wolf started to get up.

"Stay!" Nelda commanded her.

Wearing an I'll-do-it-but-I-won't-like-it expression, the wolf lay back down.

Nelda closed the bedroom door behind her and was relieved to see that the sheet on the kitchen table still reached safely to the floor. "Frick!" she said. "How nice to see you."

Frick held out a basket. "Aurelia fried some chicken for you. We were going to send Scarlet by, but there's not a sign of her."

Hopefully Gladwyn—in the bedroom, in the wardrobe— couldn't make out what they were saying. Nelda said, "That sounds like you when you were growing up: first sign of work to be done, and you were out of here."

"Just don't let her come by and pester you about that dress. May I borrow Father's ax to chop some firewood?"

"Certainly," Nelda said. "You know where I keep it in the shed."

"And I'll chop some for you tomorrow."

"Thank you."

As soon as Frick was out the door, Nelda ran back to the bedroom. "Stay," she reminded the wolf.

The wolf sighed and lowered her head yet again.

"Gladwyn," Nelda said, pulling open the wardrobe door, "it's a good thing you hid." She brought him to the window, and they were just in time to see Frick coming out of the shed with the ax. "He's looking for you," Nelda said. "He heard a rumor that you want to replace my poor dead husband in my affections, and he doesn't like that one bit."

Slowly, sounding more hopeful than sure, Gladwyn said, "Frick is of a much more easygoing nature than that."

"Except where his poor dead father is concerned."

Gladwyn still didn't look entirely convinced, but then he glanced at the bed.

The wolf was still now, but had obviously been chewing on the pillow. Goose down floated in the air currents.

"Maybe I'd better leave," Gladwyn said.

"Probably so," Nelda agreed.

As soon as Gladwyn left, Scarlet lifted up the tablecloth/ sheet. "Remind me to never again trust anything you ever say. Can I come out now, or do you have someone you don't want me to see hidden in the oven?"

"Careful of those pins in that dress," Nelda reminded her, helping her up. Then she pointed out, "I didn't tell your father you were here."

Scarlet said, "And I won't tell him about whoever it is you have stashed in the other room. Who is it?"

Nelda led Scarlet into the bedroom.

By now, the wolf had started eating the bonnet.

"Wow," Scarlet said.

Nelda said, "She's very tame. And smart. Which is more than I can say about Gladwyn. Want some dinner?"

"Sounds wonderful," Scarlet said, and the wolf must have

thought so too, because she jumped off the bed.

"I think," Nelda said, "my new friend here is all the protection I need, and as far as I'm concerned, she can stay here as long as she wants, because I like her a lot better than I like Gladwyn."

Scarlet said, "I like her, too. But Father will need a bit of convincing."

"We'll break the news to him slowly," Nelda said.

And with that, the three of them went out to the kitchen to eat up the last of the apple tarts and the fried chicken.

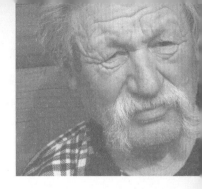

Deems the Wood Gatherer

Once upon a time, before eyeglasses were invented, there was a nearsighted but good-hearted man named Deems. Although his profession was wood gathering, what he liked most was to help others.

Since, at that time, the forests of the land were owned by the king, common folk were not allowed to chop down trees for firewood or for building. The villagers were only allowed to use trees or branches that had come down by themselves.

Wood gathering was a perfect job opportunity for Deems because, with his poor eyesight, he would have been a hazard to himself and others in many of the professions that were available to him. You wouldn't want to hand over a bow and arrow to a nearsighted archer, or a razor to a barber whose vision was blurry, or a wagonload of goods to a driver who could barely see the rump of the horse pulling the wagon— never mind being able to make out the road.

But wood was something everyone needed, and Deems was happy that his job gave him the chance to be helpful and useful. Those who knew Deems were happy, too. They were happy for the wood, and they were happy that a wood gatherer, by the king's decree, was allowed to carry only a small ax for trimming fallen branches into manageable pieces. Since—with his poor eyesight—Deems routinely failed to recognize his own children if they were across the street from him, people thought it was fortunate that Deems didn't have a tree-cutting-sized ax.

One day, after a windstorm had rattled the roofs and windows of the village the night before, Deems kissed his wife good-bye and set out for the forest to look for fallen branches.

Deems lived near woods that had a bad reputation among wood gatherers due to the odd things that happened there. Some even thought the forest had been touched by magic, with peculiar people coming and going, and with creatures making their home there who were not seen anywhere else in the wide world. There were even rumors that some of the animals knew the speech of humankind. But Deems didn't believe any of that, for he had never seen any such thing.

Of course, Deems had trouble seeing much beyond the stretch of his own arm.

So, instead of fretting, he considered himself lucky not to have to compete with the others, who avoided these woods. Working alone, he would soon and easily fill his hand-pulled cart with all the wood he needed to sell.

Today, Deems chose a path he had not gone down before and started his search. He hadn't walked long before he came to a clearing where there was a large pile of sticks and twigs. A very large pile. A pile large enough to come close to filling his wagon at one stop.

Oh, happy day! Deems thought. He gathered up all the biggest pieces, congratulating himself for this most excellent start to his work.

But while his cart was close to full, it wasn't entirely full, so Deems continued down the same path. And now he came to another clearing, and here there was a pile of lumber, every bit as high as the pile of sticks and twigs had been: boards and timbers and broken doors and window frames. *This just goes to show what's the matter with people today,* Deems thought. Someone had obviously built a house, but had not done a good job, so the house had fallen apart.

Still, even if they were too discouraged to try again, Deems thought, *they should have taken the debris to sell for scrap.*

Perhaps that wouldn't occur to someone who wasn't in the wood gathering trade. But perhaps it would. Deems decided he'd better not take this wood. Although it appeared to be abandoned, maybe someone was coming back for it. He couldn't risk the chance that he might be taking what belonged to someone else.

I will try to find my way back some other day, Deems thought, *and see if it's still here.*

The path continued, so Deems continued, since he'd had so much good luck already, and he came to another clearing, but this one had a house—a beautiful little brick house.

Deems squinted, and he saw a strange-looking fellow with a fur coat and a long nose, a fellow who was knocking on the door and saying in a sweet singsong voice, "Little pig, little pig, let me come in."

This did not strike Deems as odd, since when he and his wife were home alone, they, too, had little love names for each other. He called her "little bunny" and she called him "sweetums." Deems didn't imagine his wife would care to be called "little pig," but he suspected this man, with his outlandish full-length coat and all that facial hair, was probably a foreigner, and foreigners—of course—have foreign habits. Deems called out, "Good morrow, gentle sir. Is all well?"

The man with the long nose was so startled, he dropped to his hands and knees, in the posture of a beast. As awkward as that position must have been, he looked as if he were about to dash into the woods on all fours.

He must be embarrassed to have been overheard when he thought he was alone, Deems decided, so he said, "Sorry, my good fellow. I didn't mean to startle you. Has the missus locked you out? Sometimes my wife does that to me when she's in an irksome mood. I find that bringing her flowers often smooths things over." There happened to be a stand of wildflowers just where Deems had stopped, so he put his ax down in his cart and quickly picked a bouquet. He brought it to the long-nosed fellow, who—finally—straightened up again.

"Here you go," Deems said, handing over the flowers, because he believed one should be helpful whenever one could, even to strangers.

"Thank you," said the man Deems was thinking of as Mr. Long Nose. His voice was unusual—no doubt because of his foreign birth—soft but growly. He took the flowers, although his fingers were gnarled and clawlike—and so clumsy that he dropped several of the stems.

Arthritis, Deems speculated. With fingers like that, no wonder the poor man was reduced to knocking on his own door.

From inside the house, a high, squealy voice called out: "You can huff and you can puff all you want; you can't come in."

This struck Deems as a peculiar thing for a wife to say, even an irked wife.

Mr. Long Nose saw that Deems was puzzled. "This is not *my* house," he explained. "This is where my grandchildren live. I'm supposed to be watching over them, and they've locked me out."

Deems became aware that there were several voices coming from inside as the grandchildren continued to squeal and grunt in an overexcited way. He said, "Who knows what trouble those naughty little ones could get into." He noticed smoke coming out of the chimney. An open fire and disobedient children made for a dangerous combination. Helpfully, Deems put his shoulder to the door. Fortunately, even a brick house has a wooden door, and when he and his new friend threw their weight against it, the wood splintered. Deems could hear the children's self-satisfied laughs of glee turn into screeches of alarm. Several pairs of little feet pitter-pattered, sounding like a small herd of scattering animals.

"Don't be too hard on them," Deems told Mr. Long Nose, even though he thought the man's grandchildren acted as if they had been raised in a barn. "Children will be children."

Mr. Long Nose just smiled, showing alarming teeth (but not everyone can afford to go to a dentist regularly).

Whistling a tune popular with many wood gatherers that year, Deems continued on his way. He hadn't gone far when he ran into more ill-behaved children, although he didn't realize at first that they *were* ill-behaved. At first they just seemed to be a boy and a girl, out for a walk with their father.

"Beautiful day for a stroll with your family," Deems said.

The father grunted, and the children had nothing to say, which confirmed what Deems believed; that children should be seen and not heard.

But after the family had passed, Deems noticed that the boy had a loaf of bread under his arm, and he and the girl were breaking off small pieces of it and dropping them on the path behind them.

That's what happens when families have too much money, Deems told himself. *They don't appreciate the value of things.*

He didn't feel he should chastise the children; when they

stopped for their noonday meal, their father would soon enough realize his children had left pieces of their lunch scattered almost like a path to lead them back home.

But, because Deems felt people shouldn't litter, he picked up the pieces of bread the children had discarded.

Deems continued uphill and down, looking for those last pieces of wood to completely fill his cart.

In the afternoon, he glimpsed a child-sized red cloak between the trees, but with his bad eyesight, he couldn't be sure. He wondered if it were one of the little bread-crumb-dropping children. If so, they had walked quite far from their father.

They had better be careful, Deems thought, *or they'll get lost.*

Had that girl been wearing red? Deems couldn't remember.

A moment later, Deems heard a voice. It must have been that far away red-cloaked child, even though some strange trick of the still woods made it seem close by for all its tininess. The voice said something that sounded like: "Run, run, as fast as you can. You can't catch me, I'm the gingerbread man." Deems knew he must have misheard. The voice must have called: "Run, run, as fast as you can. Please help me catch my gingerbread man." Some small thing moved right in front of him, and Deems, guessing it was something that was being swept away by the wind, brought his foot down on it.

Sure enough, when Deems lifted his foot, what he saw

squashed on his boot was more baked goods.

Those children seemed to have no appreciation for the concept that food should not be wasted.

Even so, Deems didn't call out to the children, since they shouldn't eat food that had dropped onto the forest floor, much less food that had been stepped on. "Children today!" Deems muttered to himself as he scraped the ginger-scented dough off the bottom of his boot. "No sense at all."

By the time Deems had filled his cart with branches the previous night's storm had brought down, it was hard to pull, and the wheels creaked under the weight of the wood he had gathered. He was tired and eager to get home, so when he came to another house in a clearing, he tried to ignore the fact that the front door was wide open.

I wouldn't leave the door open like that, Deems thought. *But I never like to meddle in other people's business.*

Then he heard what sounded like "Help!" from within.

Someone in trouble was *not* something Deems could ignore.

He ran to the open doorway and called in, "What's wrong? Do you need assistance?"

No answer.

Deems stepped inside. It was an old granny's cottage; he could tell by the doilies on the chair arms and by the old-fashioned style of the used, tired looking furniture. But there was no granny. "Hello?" he called.

Someone was moving around in the other room. Then a creaky voice called, "Yes?"

"Are you in need of assistance?" Deems repeated.

"No," the creaky voice said.

Deems hesitated. "Your front door is open."

The creaky voice said, "Oh, that granddaughter of mine. Not a lick of sense. She must not have closed it behind her when she left."

"I'm coming in," Deems said. He stepped farther into the cottage. From here he could see into the second room, a bedroom with a rumpled-up bed.

And, when he approached, the world's ugliest granny.

She was lying in the bed, the covers drawn up to her hairy chin, a slightly askew bonnet on her head. "Hello, sonny," she said in her old woman's voice.

"Are you sure all is well?" Deems asked. "You don't need anything?"

"I'm fine," the granny assured him. "I've just overindulged today, with the food my granddaughter brought me." She patted her stomach. "You probably just heard me call out to myself: 'Help me stop eating before I eat everything in the house.'" She smiled, her teeth looking every bit as bad as Mr. Long Nose's, and added: "Too late." She burped, and—sure enough—the sound coming from her stomach sounded like a faint voice calling, "Help!"

"You know what's a good cure for aiding the digestion?" Deems asked. "Linden tree bark. I'll be right back." One of the last branches Deems had placed in his cart had been from a linden tree. He broke off a piece of the bark and brought it in to the granny. She was holding the pillow up against her stomach as though to stifle the unmannerly noises coming from inside it. "Chew on this," Deems told her, "and you'll be feeling like your old self in no time."

"Why, thank you, sonny," the ugly granny said.

"If you don't need anything else, I'll just close the door behind me when I leave," Deems said. "These woods are safe, but there's no point in being careless."

"No," the granny agreed. "Careless is bad. Food is good, but careless is bad."

As Deems shut the door on his way out, he wondered if she might be Mr. Long Nose's mother. *Same strange accent*, he thought.

Deems whistled as he pulled his cart. One more stop before he could head home. He had to deliver all this wood to the other old granny, the very nice old woman who lived next door to him and whose house looked and smelled like a baked treat. She had decorated it in such a child-friendly way, she had explained, because she had so many grandchildren, and she loved to bake for them. "Please bring a lot of wood," she had asked Deems that morning, "because I'm having some children over for dinner."

Deems prided himself on being observant and a good judge of character. He was happy to have accomplished so much in one day, and especially to have been such a help to so many truly nice people. Where would they be without him?

Why Willy and His Brother Won't Ever Amount to Anything

Once upon a time, after books were invented but before
TV and movies, there was a girl named Isolda Adeline
Genevieve Trenthausen. She and her several younger
brothers and sisters and her parents and her grandparents all
lived in a big house in the apple orchard her family owned.

One day in the spring, when the trees were bearing delicate
white apple blossoms and the red tasty apples of autumn were
still just a mouthwatering anticipation, Isolda was in the orchard
pulling up dandelions and wild grapevines from among the
tree roots. She had just taken off her cloak, since the morning
was getting warmer, and had set it down on the ground beside
her when she saw a sweet little baby fox. Very quietly, so as
not to make a noise that might startle the creature, Isolda sat
in the grass to make herself look smaller and less scary. Isolda

watched the fox for a few moments before the fox noticed her—and then it watched her for a few moments.

In a very soft, gentle voice Isolda said, "Hello, little one. Don't be afraid. I wouldn't hurt you." While the creature certainly couldn't understand her words, perhaps it understood her tone. Or, at the very least, it was curious. *It* took a hesitant step toward her. Then another.

Isolda had never before been this close to a fox. Her brothers and sisters were generally very noisy, and any wildlife could hear them coming from miles away. She was fortunate her siblings were nowhere nearby, for she thought the fox kit was the most beautiful thing she had ever seen, and she held her breath. Shyly, the fox took another step toward her.

Then, from behind Isolda, came the all-too-familiar voice of their neighbor, Willy. "Yah!" the young man shouted. "Get away! Scram! Leave Isolda alone!"

There was no need for more than the first word. All the others were extra. Terrified, the tiny, young fox turned its bushy tail and ran off, disappearing among the trees.

"Willy!" Isolda complained. "What did you go and do that for?"

Willy and his brother, who were a couple of years older than Isolda and her siblings, lived with their father, who was a woodcutter. Isolda's parents let the boys come to the orchard to collect fallen branches to supplement what their father gathered because—as Isolda's grandfather pointed out—both of the woodcutter's sons were dreamers who would never amount to anything, and so it was a neighborly thing to help them out. Willy said, "I rescued you."

"I didn't need rescuing," Isolda told him.

Willy snorted. "From a big, hairy wolf? I should think you did. It could have mesmerized you with its evil eyes so that you couldn't move, and then it could have torn you apart with its fearsome teeth and eaten you." Willy was always full of strange fancies and nonsensical stories.

"That wasn't a wolf," Isolda snapped. "It was a fox. A baby fox. A tiny baby fox."

"Was not."

"Yes, it was."

"Was not."

Isolda decided against arguing and instead stood and brushed the grass off her skirt.

"Are you sure?" Willy asked.

"Absolutely."

Sulking a bit, Willy grumbled, "Well, it could have had rabies." With a little too much enthusiasm, he added, "It could have bitten you, and then in a few days you would have started foaming at the mouth, and you'd be trying to bite people yourself, and then you'd have convulsions, and then you'd become paralyzed, and then you'd die."

"Good-bye, Willy," Isolda said. She started to walk away.

"Isolda!" Willy called. "You forgot your red cloak."

Isolda rolled her eyes before she turned around. Everyone knew that, among Willy's other disadvantages, he was color-blind. She didn't point out to him that her cloak was green, not red. Maybe it was his color blindness that was responsible for his confusing a brown fox for a gray wolf. Of course, that didn't take into account the difference between a fox and a wolf in size, face, tail, or demeanor. More likely, Willy was simply letting his imagination run away with him. Again.

"Thank you, Willy," she said, without commenting that Willy's dirty hands had left smudges all over her cloak. Then, because she was a kind girl, she added, "If the day gets hot and you and your brother need a drink of water, come up to the house."

"Thank you, Isolda," Willy said.

Then, because Isolda was kind, not a saint, she moved to another section of the orchard to do her weeding.

By noon, neither Willy nor his brother had stopped by the house, which was unusual, for they both liked talking better than working. After Isolda had helped her mother get all the brothers and sisters cleaned up before lunch, and then fed them lunch, and cleaned them up after lunch, Isolda heard her grandmother say, "I need a little help with the sewing project I've been working on."

Isolda's brothers and sisters ran out of the house before they, too, could be asked to help.

Isolda followed her grandmother into the parlor. On the

table was Grandmother's sewing basket, as well as pincushions, and piles of fabric, and cotton batting for stuffing. There was also a bucket that was full of small stones.

"This past winter," Grandmother said, "I was so plagued by drafts coming in from under the doors and windows, that I ended up stuffing rags in the cracks."

"Yes," Isolda said. It would have been hard not to notice.

"What I'm trying to do," Grandmother explained, "is make something we can use next winter that will look a little nicer. I thought I could fashion something attractive, as well as useful. So I made this for your brother Josef's room." Grandmother opened the sewing basket and pulled out a long, fat calico snake.

"It's adorable!" Isolda cried. "Josef will love it!"

"It's stuffed with stones," Grandmother explained, "so that it stays in place, but I've wrapped the stones with the batting, so that it's soft and not lumpy."

"Grandmother, you're brilliant!" Isolda said.

"Well, it's a little early for you to say that," Grandmother said. "A snake was a natural, with its long, skinny body. So was a caterpillar, which I made for Franz." Grandmother once again opened the basket, and this time she pulled out a green, segmented stuffed animal, complete with wire antennae.

"That's the sweetest thing I've ever seen!" Isolda cried.

"Next, I made a trout for Leopold." Grandmother had fashioned this animal with tiny scallops of fabric that had a sheen to them, to look like fish scales.

"Ooh," Isolda cooed.

"But then . . ." Grandmother added before Isolda could repeat that Grandmother was brilliant, ". . . then I decided to make this for Rutger." Grandmother pulled some gray, furry fabric out of her basket.

Hesitantly, Isolda said, "Well, that's cute . . ."

But she needed her grandmother to explain, "It's a wolf," before Isolda got it.

"Yes," Isolda said. "I can see that now." She could, if she squinted a bit.

"The head is wrong," Grandmother said.

"It's stylized," Isolda said.

Grandmother said, "It's just wrong. But I've been working on it too long, and I can't see what I need to do."

"Well . . ." Isolda didn't like to criticize, but Grandmother was asking for her advice.

"He's fine the way he is, but if you want to make him more realistic, Grandmother, his eyes are too big."

"The better to see you with." Grandmother laughed. "But I can make them smaller."

"And, Grandmother, his ears are too big."

"The better to hear you with," Grandmother said. "But that's easy to fix."

"And, Grandmother, his arms are too big."

"The better to hug you with," Grandmother answered. "But

I see what you mean."

"And, Grandmother, his teeth are too big."

"The better to eat you with!" Grandmother playfully moved the stuffed animal toward Isolda as if it were a real wolf, lunging. From behind them, a voice called, "Fear not! I will rescue both of you!" And in another moment, helpful neighbor Willy dashed into the room. He yanked Grandmother's handiwork away from her and threw it down on the floor. In less time than it takes to blink—so before either Grandmother or Isolda could utter a word—Willy had his woodcutting hatchet unfastened from his belt, and he swung it hard, splitting the not-quite-a-wolf draft-stopper Grandmother had sewn.

Isolda and her grandmother looked at Willy, speechless. Bits of stuffing wafted in the air currents.

Isolda could see Jakob, hovering in the kitchen doorway, as seriously confused as his brother Willy, but not so brave.

After a long, long, long moment, Willy said, "Oh." Then he said to Isolda, "You told me that we could come in for some water."

"So I did," Isolda said.

Willy continued to look at the ripped wolf on the floor, with its stones and its stuffing spilling out. Not exactly apologizing—Willy was not the sort of person to ever apologize—he explained: "We were in the kitchen, Jakob and me, and we heard you in here. We couldn't see you, Ma'am, because the settee blocked the way. But we saw that . . . that . . . thing there, and Jakob said, 'What if it's a wolf?' And I said, 'What if it's a talking, enchanted wolf that's trying to convince Isolda that it's her grandmother?' And Jakob said, 'What if it's eaten her grandmother, and it's about to eat Isolda?'"

Grandmother was too kind a person to tell him what she really thought. "Well, we're fine now," she assured the two brothers.

"Good." Willy tipped his hat at her. "Ma'am," he said. "Isolda."

Isolda and her grandmother silently watched until Willy had backed out of the room, taking Jakob with him.

"It's difficult to tell which of those brothers is more foolish," Grandmother whispered to Isolda, "Jakob or Wilhelm. They live in a fantasy world of their own."

Shaking her head, Isolda agreed. "Those Grimm brothers," she said with a sigh, "they'll never amount to anything."

And she was right because all they ever became was writers.

The Little Red Headache

Once upon a time, before superhighways and hotel chains, a wolf was journeying through the woods. He paused to take a nap and was awakened when someone stepped on his tail. It wasn't the waking up that was the problem: The wolf's sleep had been fitful, disturbed by a nightmare involving three singing pigs who repeatedly invited him into their house, only to slam their front door in his face. The wolf would have been happy enough to have that dream interrupted. But the sudden sharp pain from a foot coming down on his tail brought him to his feet—all four of them—with a startled yowl. Still sleep-dazed, he would not have been surprised to find that the mean-spirited pigs were real after all and the source of the throbbing in his tail.

But it was not spiteful pigs with big, heavy feet that had awakened him; it was a human girl.

Upon seeing the wolf springing up right in front of her, the girl screeched in terror, an earsplitting cry that made the wolf instantly forget the ache in his tail for the new ache that seared through his brain.

He clapped his front paws over his ears, but that did little to diminish the volume—and nothing to diminish the shrillness—of the child's shrieks.

Fortunately the girl had more defenses than the annoyingly piercing voice. She ran. Away. She zigzagged among the trees, her red cloak flapping behind her. The wolf couldn't understand humans and their fondness for covering the bodies that God had given them with fabrics or (shudder!) the skins of other animals. But surely the girl's cloak was unattractive even by human standards: a color and texture and shape unlike anything found in nature, and having an unfortunate tendency to snag itself on tree bark and bush branches as the girl fled. The wolf concluded that the girl's family must not be able to provide for her—a condition humans called *poor*, which could mean without material possessions, as well as pitiable—and that she had to settle for the hideous red garment or go cold.

As the wolf was starting to feel sorry for the girl, he noticed that in her fright she had dropped a basket. She must have been gathering flowers, for daisies and alyssum and morning glories were spilling out of it onto the ground. Overlaying the scent of the flowers came the aromas of smoked venison, carrots, strawberries, and—as far as the wolf was concerned, the single best thing human beings had ever invented—fresh-baked bread.

The wolf inhaled deeply the tantalizing smells of meat and baked goods, and was strongly tempted to gobble everything up. But his mother had raised him better than that.

"Little girl!" he called after the fleeing child. He could no longer see her, though her shrieks trailed behind her like a rat's tail. "You forgot your food!"

Apparently the little girl could not understand wolf speech any more than the wolf could understand human speech, since she didn't come back.

If the wolf hadn't had such a deeply held moral belief system, he could have convinced himself that by leaving the basket behind, the girl had forsaken her rights to it. But, instead, he picked up the basket in his teeth, then loped through the trees, following the trails of wailing, crushed forest vegetation and human scent.

He soon came within sight of the girl, who had gotten herself wedged between two close-together bushes. Her cries had moderated to a low whine until she caught sight of him again.

Despite her screeches, which made the wolf's eyes cross, he set the basket down and went to free the girl from the grasping greenery. With his teeth, he took hold of the edge of the cloak. Unfortunately, the wool cloak tasted so much like sheep that for a moment—just a moment—he forgot himself, and took a bite of it.

Still, that was no reason for the girl to carry on as though he'd taken a bite out of her. "Sorry," the wolf told her, "I lost my head. On the other hand, you might notice that I did get you loose."

But, of course, he said this in wolf, not human, and the girl apparently did not pick up on the apologetic tone.

With another intense squeal, she ran away again.

Well, the wolf thought, *now both my head and my tail are aching. And she STILL left the basket behind.*

The wolf considered what he should do.

His rumbling stomach tried to convince his better judgment that maybe the basket didn't belong to the girl after all, and that was why she kept leaving it behind when she ran off. Maybe these were two separate things: the basket had ended up beside him, and the girl had trod on his tail—but neither incident had anything to do with the other.

That must be it, the wolf's stomach insisted.

But if that's the case, the wolf asked his stomach, *then who does the basket belong to?*

His stomach practically shouted: US! *It belongs to us!* But the wolf considered again the life lessons learned at his mother's four knees. And then he started to remember the forest cottage he'd noticed that morning shortly before he'd fallen asleep. Maybe whoever lived there had been the one to drop the basket. The cottage was very close to where he'd settled down for his nap, and come to think of it, maybe it was seeing that cottage that had given him the nightmare about the taunting pigs.

I'll bring the basket to the cottage, the wolf told his

stomach. *But if it turns out that pigs live there, then I'll keep the basket, to make up for the bad dream.*

His stomach wasn't happy, but—then again—neither were his tail nor his head.

The wolf once more picked the basket up with his teeth, and he made his way to the cottage he'd seen earlier.

The cottage sat in a little clearing surrounded by flowers. That was another odd thing about humans: They would take a section of ground and clear away all the flowers that grew there already all on their own, and then they would plant a whole other assortment of flowers in their place. This seemed like a lot of pointless effort to the wolf, but humans weren't alone in that regard: other animals, too, engaged in behavior that struck the wolf as meaningless. Like squirrels, with their running up and down trees all the time, burying nuts and then digging them up again. And what about fish, who spent all day swimming and never came out of the water to dry off? It was beyond understanding.

The wolf sniffed beneath the door just to be sure this was a human cottage. The scent was undeniable. No pigs, except in bacon form. The wolf thought being in bacon form was a very sensible way for pigs to behave.

Now, the wolf knew that some of his dog cousins who lived with people had trained their humans to open doors for them, because dogs, like wolves, have paws that are excellently well suited for doing many things, but opening doors is not one of them. So the wolf sat at the door of the cottage and scratched at the wood with his claws.

After a little bit, he heard a human voice call out from inside the house, "Little Red Riding Hood, is that you? Have you come to visit your Granny?" But since the wolf didn't speak human, he guessed that what the person had said was: "Did I hear something? If there's someone out there who needs to come in, could you please scratch louder?"

So that's what the wolf did: he scratched louder.

With his own very finely attuned ears, he heard the person who was inside the cottage walk toward the door.

Still holding the basket handle in his teeth, the wolf tried to smile in a friendly manner, and at the same time—as soon as the door opened—he stepped forward and asked, "Is this your basket? I found it in the woods nearby, and if it's yours, I'm certainly willing to hand it over, because that's the right thing to do; although I have to admit I'm rather hoping that it's not yours, because it smells truly delicious, and I would very much like to eat the good things packed in it. Though of course I'd be willing to share. I'm especially willing to share the fruits and vegetables and flowers."

The old lady who had opened her door to find a grinning wolf on her step did not speak wolf. Still, somehow or other she correctly interpreted that his growling had something to do with his intention to eat. Unfortunately, what she deduced he intended to eat was her.

She shrieked with such a shrillness that the wolf guessed that she was related to the screeching child he'd already met; however, he was soon distracted by the old woman trying to slam the door shut. Just like the pigs in his dream!

But, because the wolf had taken a step forward, the door simply bounced off the edge of the basket he was holding in his muzzle, jarring his teeth, and yet leaving the way wide open.

"Is that a 'yes' or a 'no'?" the wolf asked as the old lady turned and ran back into the room.

Without answering, the old lady ran around her bed and opened another door that was on a box as tall as she was, and as wide. The wolf caught a glimpse of a small room that was full of clothing before the old lady stepped into the box and pulled the door shut behind her.

Abandoning someone who had come to visit struck the wolf as bordering upon being rude, but he continued to mind his own manners.

The wolf said, "I'm taking it that means 'no.' All right?" He waited for a few moments, but there was no answer.

Was the box/room where she kept her bacon? Was she in there, eating the bacon all up, so she didn't have to share?

The wolf set the basket down on the floor and ate the venison and the loaf of bread, which were both as delicious as they smelled. Occasionally he paused to say, "You're missing out on a real treat." But he couldn't bring himself to say it very loudly, and maybe that was why the old lady still wouldn't come out.

"Well," the wolf finally told her when he was done, "I'm leaving the basket and the flora and the produce. Enjoy!" He tried to sound enthusiastic, in the hope of making the daisies and the strawberries and the carrots sound like worthwhile things.

But just then he heard someone approaching from the outside. "Granny!" a human voice called. "Granny, are you home?" It was the little human girl; he could tell by the way his headache was threatening to blow up inside his skull at the sound of her voice.

Oh, no! the wolf thought. *It was her basket after all! And now I've gone and eaten all the best parts.*

The cottage was so small, there was no place to hide.

Except . . .

The wolf jumped onto the bed and burrowed under the covers. The wolf was aware of the girl approaching the bed and talking, talking, talking.

For a while he thought, *Well, at least she isn't shouting.* But even in this quieter tone, her voice hurt his head. He moaned, but that just seemed to encourage the child: She would say something, he would moan, and then she would say something else as though he'd answered her. Eventually, he could stand it no longer and he peeked out from beneath the blanket and tried to explain how he hadn't meant to eat all the goodies in the basket.

But at the sight of him, the girl began that high-pitched screaming noise. For whatever reason, that got the old lady in her little box/room to finally make her presence known, too. The wolf suspected the old lady was inviting the girl to join her in the box/room to eat some bacon. Both voices reverberated in the wolf's brain until his patience snapped.

"You're worse than the pigs!" he told them. "No manners at all!"

And, with that, he jumped out of the bed and ran out of the cottage. On the front step he collided with a man carrying an ax over his shoulder. The man yelled, "It's a wolf! Granny, save me!" but the wolf had had enough of people and their nonsensical ways, and he didn't even try to decipher the man's words.

Because the wolf didn't stay, he never heard the story people ended up telling about him.

But, then again, because the wolf didn't stay, people never heard the story the wolf told about them.

Little Red Riding Hood's Little Red Riding Hood

Once upon a time, before malls, boutiques, or online clothing catalogs, there was a fairy godmother who was having trouble finding something to wear to the naming-day ceremony for her goddaughter.

"This dress makes me look fat," the fairy godmother muttered to herself as she rummaged through her closet.

"That one has a stain on it."

"This top looks as if it should go with this skirt, but it does not."

And: "What was I thinking when I bought *that*?"

Nothing suited her, but she did not want to use magic to give herself a new outfit or to alter what she already had because—at her age—she could manage only one good magic spell per day, and she was saving that wish to bestow on the godchild.

"Oh, for goodness' sake!" she said, pulling out a dress she hadn't worn in several years. "This will have to do."

There were, of course, reasons she hadn't worn it in several years: The top was too tight, the sleeves were too full, and the skirt had a snagged thread right over her belly. Still, for the moment, it was the least objectionable outfit she could find.

Besides, thought the fairy godmother, her cloak would cover up most of the dress. The family she was going to visit lived in a little cottage in the woods, which meant there probably would be drafts: a good excuse to leave the cloak on, even indoors.

However, on this particular day, even the cloak didn't please her.

Why had she ever chosen such a bright red dye to color it?

Why had she made it so long?

Why had she attached that awful hood?

The fairy godmother scowled at her reflection in the mirror. Worn up, the hood was big and floppy around her face, as if the fabric had stretched, or her head had shrunk; down, it was lumpy and bulky across her shoulders, making her look hunchbacked.

And, on top of everything else, the wool was scratchy around her face.

And yet it would have to do, since she was already going to be late for the baby's naming.

The fairy godmother rushed out of her house, and the cloak caught in the door as she slammed it behind her. Although she had once liked the way the cloak swished dramatically around her ankles, now she regretted ever making the miserable thing in the first place.

As she had feared, she indeed was late for the gathering, despite the fact that she practically ran all the way. When she arrived, flustered and slightly out of breath, with twigs and leaves and forest debris clinging to her hem, she found that most of the feast-day food had already been eaten. Worse, the priest had already come and gone, and the child had been baptized Ruby Marie. It was not a name the fairy godmother would have ever chosen, but nobody was interested in hearing the list of suggestions she had been drawing up over the last several months.

"So nice to see you, dear," the child's father said, but then with the next breath he announced that he, too, was about to leave. He needed to walk his mother-in-law home since she lived quite some distance through the woods and she wanted to travel while it was still light out, for fear of the wolves who lived in the area. So the fairy godmother was put on the spot to announce her gift right away.

She had weighed several traditional options as she trekked

through the woods. Beauty? That was superficial. Wealth could be a trap. A gentle spirit was often taken advantage of. She had thought long and seriously about all this and had decided that what would benefit the child most would be smartness. Someone who was smart could make her way in the world, no matter what her looks or what her economic circumstances.

However, something else had been on the fairy godmother's mind as she had walked to the cottage: What a nuisance that silly red cloak of hers was. It bunched where it should lay flat, rubbed a rash onto her neck, caught on things, wasn't warm enough out in the woods, and was too warm in the cottage. *Stupid cloak!* she had thought several times.

She tried to put all those fashion thoughts aside as she leaned over Ruby Marie's cradle. She emptied her mind and gathered the magic to her, then released it. "I wish . . ." she started.

Because she was leaning, the hem of the front of her cloak was pooled onto the floor at her feet. Someone in the crowd, moving in for a closer view, stepped on it, yanking the fairy godmother's head down. Her forehead smacked the wooden edge of the cradle.

Stupid cloak! Why couldn't it fit properly and swish only when she wanted it to swish and be attractive in a way to fit her every mood?

Distracted by that thought, the fairy godmother rubbed the

sore spot on her forehead and heard her own voice say, "I wish this cloak . . ."

No, no, no! Not the cloak! The child! She was supposed to be wishing for the child to be smart!

So that's what she said: ". . . to be smart. Ouch." She could feel the bump already starting on her head.

She heard the party guests murmuring.

And she realized what she had done. She had just wished smartness not onto the godchild, but onto the cloak.

I wish, she thought to herself, *I wasn't such an idiot.*

But she had already used her wish for the day, so absolutely nothing changed.

There wasn't anything to be done, so the fairy godmother pulled off the cloak and laid it in little Ruby Marie's cradle—as if that had been her intention all along.

The cloak, clever article of clothing that it now was, immediately fitted itself around the sleeping baby, just the right size to tuck itself about her, just the right weight to keep her warm but not overheated, just the right softness to make her feel safe and to give her cozy dreams.

"Enjoy," the fairy godmother said.

Then she got out of there, fast, before anyone could comment on the ugly out-of-style dress she was wearing.

As the years passed, the cloak grew and shifted to fit Ruby Marie's needs. In fact, by the time the child was twelve years old, most people didn't even call her Ruby Marie anymore, but Little Red Riding Hood, because . . . well, because the girl wasn't the most pleasant or stimulating person, and the magical cloak was the most interesting thing about her.

However, while people recognized that the cloak was smart in a stylish sense, and that it fit the child as well as it had fit the baby, and that it always draped perfectly and never dragged on the floor nor snagged on pieces of furniture, and that it needed neither cleaning nor mending nor ironing, and that it was always just the right thickness and weight, and that the red transformed itself brighter or deeper to fit Little Red Riding Hood's whim—despite all this, no one took into account the full extent of the fairy godmother's spell. For while the fairy godmother had wished for the cloak to be smart, she had not granted it the gift of speech. So none of those who routinely praised the cloak's durability and versatility and appearance—not a one—realized how truly smart the cloak actually was.

And this was especially the case for Little Red, who, truth be told, could have used some of that smartness spell herself.

As could her mother, which may indeed have been how the fairy godmother had come to think that smartness was a good gift idea to begin with.

"Little Red Riding Hood," the mother called one beautiful spring day.

The cloak cringed, its edges curling up in distaste, thinking, as it always did, that "Little Red Riding Hood" would have been a perfectly fine name for itself (even though it wasn't always little, and wasn't always a riding hood, though it was—generally speaking—red); but for a child, the name was totally inappropriate.

"Yes, Mother," the girl answered, sounding simultaneously bored and annoyed at being interrupted. But at least she didn't sound angry. Little Red could have quite a temper.

"Your grandmama has a terrible cold and is confined to bed, so I thought it would be nice for you to go and visit her, and for you to take her this tasty supper I prepared, so she can concentrate on resting and getting better."

The cloak couldn't believe its . . . well, it didn't have ears, but it couldn't believe the fibers it listened with. *Haven't you ever heard of germs?* it wanted to shout. *Don't you know that you're endangering your offspring? Is the concept of contagion beyond you?*

But, this being before the time of Louis Pasteur and the discovery of germs, she hadn't, she didn't, and it was.

The only reason the cloak knew was because it was so smart.

Little Red Riding Hood had been sitting at the window, wearing her cloak because it made her feel attractive. She was gazing out into the yard without really seeing what was there—or at least not seeing the vegetable garden that needed weeding nor the fence that could have used a fresh coat of paint nor the patch of herbs that was rather desperate for watering. Her mind drifted as she wondered how to fill this long day, since she did not have a very good imagination and had trouble coming up with ideas about how to amuse herself. Even so, she sighed, loudly, at her mother's request. "I suppose . . ." she grumbled, "if I really *have* to," as though this errand was tearing her away from things she absolutely needed to do.

"Thank you," the mother said, handing a cloth-covered basket to Little Red. "Go directly there, and don't stop to talk to strangers on the way."

If the cloak had only had vocal cords, it could have said: *Hel-lo-o! Strangers? You're worried about STRANGERS? No strangers ever come into these woods. There are too many WOLVES around that scare any self-respecting strangers away!* The cloak had never had a mother, but it knew Little Red's mother was in desperate need of a remedial course in parenting.

"All right, all right," Little Red told her mother. "I'm not a child."

Even though she was.

The cloak tried to grab hold of the door frame to slow the girl down. The cloak hoped that if Little Red's father happened to come by, at least he might know enough not to send a not-very-bright twelve-year-old girl out into wolf-infested woods with only a basket of baked goods and a red cloak for protection.

But the father was busy doing whatever it was that he was

doing, and Little Red tugged the cloak loose from the door frame, saying, "Stupid cloak," which was the single most unfair thing she could have said.

Despite her mother's instructions to go directly to her grandmother's house, Little Red walked slowly, scuffing her shoes in the dust and muttering to herself.

The cloak tried to rush her along, pulling at her as if a wind blew from behind, but the girl couldn't be hurried. In fact, she stopped to pick daisies, which she then sat down to weave into a flower crown for herself.

The red cloak toned down its color so as not to attract attention, but not much time had passed before it became aware of some movement between the trees off to the right of the path. If the cloak could have uttered a single sound, it would have been, "Shhh," for Little Red was singing a loud song about finding her true love. *You're twelve,* the cloak wanted to tell her. *There will be plenty of time for finding your true love IF you don't get yourself eaten before then.*

The creature that had been angling off to the east now turned back and stepped onto the path in front of Little Red.

It was, as the cloak had feared, a wolf. Worse than that, it was a wolf standing on its hind legs. Then, as now, that was pretty unusual for wolves. Worst of all, the wolf said, "Hello, hello. What's a sweet morsel of a girl like you doing all alone in the woods?"—which was not only unusual, it was a bit creepy.

Obviously, the cloak thought, *this talking wolf must be*

the product of some science experiment. Either that, or a magic spell.

It was hard to think that much good could come of the situation, whatever the animal's background.

Little Red, however, did not seem to be aware that there were all sorts of reasons to be alarmed.

"What I'm doing," she said, only glancing up for a moment from her work with the daisies, "should be obvious even to a great lummox like you: I'm making a daisy crown."

Not for the first time, the cloak wished that the fairy godmother would come back and hit the child with a politeness spell. *No, no, no,* the cloak wished it could say to Little Red. *Don't antagonize the beast!*

However, the wolf didn't seem to take offense. He said, "So you're trying to prettify yourself for your young man, then? Not that you need to: you're already as pretty as a succulent lamb in spring. Where is your lucky fellow—roaming the nearby woods, checking to make sure the surroundings are safe for you?"

Little Red snorted. "As if. I'm perfectly capable of taking care of myself."

The cloak fluttered up to cover her mouth to keep her from admitting that she was all alone, but the wolf apparently didn't need a smartness spell to help him figure that out.

"All by yourself, are you, then, my savory flightless bird, smelling so delicious?"

That, finally, seemed to get Little Red's attention.

But the wolf pointed to the basket she had put down on the ground beside her. "Fresh pork with a dash of rosemary; roasted potatoes with sage; hard-boiled eggs—two? No, three of them—still in their shells; turnips and onions in vinaigrette; and a blueberry tart with just a hint of lemon."

Reassured, Little Red pulled the cloak down from covering her mouth and said, "You have a very good nose."

"It's a gift," the wolf said modestly. "So, all that scrumptious food for a tasty tidbit of a girl like you?"

Little Red answered, "It's for my grandmother."

"She lives nearby, does she, you yummy, young rabbit of a girl?" the wolf asked. "Within, just for an example, calling distance?"

"I wish!" Little Red said. "No, I've got to go tromping through these woods for a good hour to get there."

Won't this child EVER stop talking? the cloak wondered, once again trying to gag her, but this time Little Red was prepared. She yanked the cloak away from her face and shoved as much of it as she could beneath her so that, by sitting on it, she could keep it in place.

"No granddad to help out, my tempting tenderloin of delectability?" the wolf asked.

"No," Little Red said. "He died years ago. Now my mother's sent me because Granny is old and sick and feeble and barely able to move. Totally helpless. I have to do everything for her."

Then, with a cry of exasperation as the cloak yanked itself out from under her and once again tried to muffle her words, she demanded, "What is it with this cloak? It's trying to strangle me!" She jumped to her feet and unfastened it, but the cloak clung to her anyway, frantic to shush her, for her safety was its responsibility.

"Help!" Little Red cried.

The ever-helpful wolf grabbed hold of the cloak with his claws, ripped it off her body, and threw it to the ground.

"Thank you," Little Red said, apparently totally oblivious to the way the wolf, now standing close enough to begin devouring her, was licking his lips.

But in the next moment, Little Red realized that the wolf's sharp nails had not only pulled the cloak off her, they had ripped the fabric. She smacked the wolf's muzzle, hard. "You stupid animal!" she shouted. "Stupid, stupid, stupid." With each *stupid,* she hit his delicate nose again.

The wolf backed away, his muzzle stinging.

Little Red picked up the cloak and hugged it close to her. "This was my favorite article of clothing," she yelled at the wolf. "This was special. Any fool could have seen that. But nooooo, not you, you common, stupid . . . beast, you!"

The cloak, which had been about to repair itself, was smart enough to hesitate. Instead, it gave a weak flutter, as if its wounds were beyond its ability to heal, but as if it were bravely trying.

The wolf protested, "I am not stupid, sweetmeat. You *asked* me to help."

But Little Red talked right over him, saying, "I bet your own mother was sorry she ever had a stupid excuse of a lunkbrain like you."

Ooh, the cloak thought. *That's harsh.*

The wolf looked simultaneously hurt and resentful. He took a step closer to Little Red—but retreated again when she raised her hand in the direction of his muzzle. He said, "But, pork chop, you're the one—"

"Stop making excuses!"

"But—"

Little Red covered her ears and said in a singsong voice, "I'm not listening. I'm not listening."

This was annoying enough that the wolf looked as if he might seriously consider risking another whack on the nose.

But instead—summoning all his dignity—he said, "I am not stupid." And he dropped to all fours and trotted back toward the woods.

Providing a strong hint that she *was* listening after all, Little Red called after him: "Yes, you are."

Right before the wolf slunk from sight, the cloak heard him mutter, "I'll show you who's stupid," which caused the cloak to shiver. But Little Red had resumed chanting, "I'm not listening."

Once the wolf was gone, Little Red put the cloak back on.

The cloak fixed the place where the wolf's claws had torn it, which it supposed made Little Red happy, but the girl certainly didn't say so. She picked up the flower crown and finished making it before taking up the basket and starting once again down the path to her grandmother's cottage.

When they got there, the cloak was alarmed to see that the front door was wide open. The cloak spread itself out, billowing like a sail, trying to slow Little Red, to give her time to take note of this out-of-the-ordinary detail, which, as far as the cloak was concerned, screamed *Danger!*

But Little Red said, "Don't start this nonsense again," and held her elbows tight against her body to keep the cloak close so that it couldn't grab at the doorway.

Little Red swept into the house, calling out, "Granny!" and not using what her parents would have termed "an indoors voice," and not taking into account that the ailing old woman might have been taking a nap.

"In here, cupcake," came a creaky voice from the other room.

That's odd, the cloak thought, *even if she has a sore throat, that doesn't sound like Little Red's grandmother. And when has she ever called Little Red "cupcake"?*

But Little Red was not suspicious, only rude. She took barely two steps into the house and shouted, "I'm leaving a basket of goodies by the door for you, Granny. Hope you're feeling better soon. Bye."

"Wait!" the voice called. "My little *bonbon* of tasty perfection! Come in and visit with me for a bit."

The voice . . . the tone . . . the figures of speech . . . *No!* the cloak wanted to yell.

But, of course, the cloak couldn't talk.

Little Red sighed loudly. Probably loudly enough to be heard in the other room. She muttered, "Take up my whole day, why don't you?" But, stomping her feet, which, by the way, loosened clumps of dirt from the bottoms of her shoes and left them in little piles on the previously clean floor, Little Red walked to the bedroom door.

The cloak fluttered anxiously at the sight of the figure in the bed. *Wolf!* it sang out with every fiber of wool in its body.

Wolf! Wolf! Wolf!

Wolf in grandmother's clothes!

Wolf!

But, unfortunately, wool fiber is not very loud at all. The cloak caught hold of the doorway, although this had yet to prove to be a useful tactic. Little Red Riding Hood threw all her weight into moving forward, so that when she broke the cloak's grip, she catapulted herself into the room, and in a moment she was more than halfway to the bed, where the wolf was waiting.

"Geez, Granny!" Little Red exclaimed. "You *are* sick, aren't you? You look awful. Your eyes are all . . ."–Little Red grimaced–". . . yellow."

"Ooh," said the wolf in the grandmother's clothes, "come closer and let these poor old eyes of mine feast on you, you little treat, you."

The cloak flapped, but Little Red weighed too much to become airborne.

Little Red walked right up to the bed. "Geez, Granny," she said. "Your ears are all hairy."

The wolf tried to sound apologetic. "That happens when people get old, my apple tart of a girl. Come closer."

The cloak pushed against the bed, trying to force Little Red backwards.

Little Red couldn't be stopped. "And, geez, Granny, it smells like wet dog in here."

The wolf said, "My dear little mouthwatering snack, I've been sick as a dog and unable to clean myself or the room. But I have something here for you."

The cloak could hear a noise coming from the cupboard on the other side of the room: a banging sound, as if someone was trapped inside. A grandmotherly voice—a *real* grandmotherly voice, although muffled from being inside—cried out, "Run, Little Red! Run!"

But Little Red was concentrating on the wolf grand-mother's promise of "something here for you." Still, she couldn't help but say as she leaned over the bed, "And, geez, Granny, your teeth have gotten *so* nasty."

Dropping all pretense of grandmotherhood, the wolf

lunged, growling, "Who's the stupid one now, you appetizing little entrée? Those teeth are to eat you with!"

The cloak swung around and threw itself across the wolf's face.

Temporarily blinded, the wolf fell back onto the bed.

Little Red, who had long ago missed out on that smartness spell, said, "Where is it, Granny? What do you have for me? I can't see—the cloak is in the way." She tried to pull the cloak free, off the wolf's face.

The cloak flipped itself over and off Little Red's body and totally onto the wolf.

"Let go, you stupid cloak!" Little Red shouted. "You're smothering Granny before she can give me my present."

The cloak was not smothering the wolf, just holding him down to give Little Red the chance to escape. Because the fairy godmother had presented the cloak to Little Red, the cloak belonged to her and had to protect her, even if it got torn and shredded beyond its ability to repair itself.

The wolf began to howl; the actual grandmother in the cupboard found something to bang against the door—it sounded like a big metal bowl—and Little Red raised her voice to be heard over the commotion.

"I hate you!" she screamed at the cloak. "I wish the fairy godmother had never given you to me! Let go of my granny!"

From outside the house, a man's voice called, "What's going on in there? Do you need help?"

"Yes!" Little Red screamed. "Help! Murder! Help!"

The wolf realized that the last thing he needed was some-one in the room who wasn't:

a) helpless

or

b) clueless.

So, with the cloak still covering his face and tangling his legs, he clawed his way blindly to the window and jumped out.

Once the wolf was no longer in the house, the cloak let go, and settled down into a heap beneath the window.

From indoors came the sound of the man's heavy boots as he ran into the house and to the bedroom. "What's happened?" he asked.

The cloak heard Little Red say, "My granny. She's gone."

From inside the cupboard, the grandmother banged the bowl.

The man must have opened the cupboard door, for his voice cheerily announced, "Well, here she is."

"That's the wrong granny!" Little Red snapped at him. "You great, stupid clod. You scared away my other granny, who had something for me."

The cloak had heard enough, and it had had enough. By saying "I wish the fairy godmother had never given you to me," Little Red had clearly given up her claim to ownership. The cloak was no longer bound to her. It lifted itself up a hand span or so from the ground, then pulled itself a few inches along the lawn. Over and over. Sort of like how a snake might move if it were totally flat.

But it *was* moving, and eventually it got itself out of the clearing, before anyone could come looking for it. The last thing the cloak heard was Little Red asking her grandmother, "Well, do *you* have anything for me?"

The cloak did finally make it away from that cottage. It was found by a person who kept if for a while, and then passed it on to another person. And then another, and another—because the cloak was smart enough to never again show exactly how smart it was.

Eventually, a long time later, the smart red cloak ended up being found by a certain superhero in the 20th century, where it helped its new owner leap tall buildings in a single bound, and get through a whole new series of adventures.

But that's a different story.